THE MOON CHASER

ALEXA KANG

ISBN: 978-1082489396

Cover art by Keri Knutson
https://www.alchemybookcovers.com

❀ Created with Vellum

This story was originally published as part of the USA Today Bestselling WWII anthology *The Darkest Hour: Tales of WWII Resistance*.

CONTENTS

List of Main Characters

Note: Surnames of Chinese characters are placed first except when shown last and separated by comma.

Wen-Ying, Yuan - Member of resistance group Tian Di Hui (the Heaven and Earth Society). She ranks fourth in the Shanghai branch of Tian Di Hui and thus holds the honored title of "Golden Phoenix" of their branch. Her primary responsibility is to intercept radio communications and to translate intelligence and confidential documents.

Masao Takeda (aka Zheng-Xiong), **Takeda** is the surname - Half-Chinese, half-Japanese member of Tian Di Hui who is a double agent. He supports Tian Di Hui as an undercover by working for the Japanese military. In *Kanji,* the Chinese words adopted into the Japanese language, **Masao** is written and read as **Zheng-Xiong** in Chinese.

Fan Yong Hao/Fan Da Ge - Leader of the Shanghai branch of Tian Di Hui (honored title "First Helm"). He is addressed by the resistance group members as **Fan Da Ge**; *Da Ge* in Chinese means eldest brother.

Dai Li - Head of *Juntong,* the Chinese secret police of the actual Chinese regime at war with Japan. Collaborates with Tian Di Hui in resistance missions.

Secondary Characters in Alphabetical Order
(Minor characters excluded)

Bao Gong - The hired cook of collaborators Liu Kun and Shen Yi. He is a secret supporter of the resistance.

Dr. Wu Zhan Ping - Elderly doctor who provides a hidden place in his medical clinic for Tian Di Hui members to meet in secret.

Huang Jia-Ming - The third highest ranking member of the Shanghai branch of Tian Di Hui (honored title "Third Home Guard".)

Lian jie - Dr. Wu's wife. In Chinese, *jie* is the honorific for addressing an older sister or someone who the speakers and other respected as such.

Liu Kun - Japanese collaborator who would become the new occupant of Yuan Wen-Ying's old ancestral home in Shanghai.

Mei Mei - Yuan Wen-Ying's younger sister who is now deceased. (She is referred to but does not appear in this story.)

Shen Yi - Wife of Japanese collaborator Liu Kun. Former fiancée of Yuan Wen-Ying's older brother Yuan Guo-Hui.

Tang Wei - Secretary of Propaganda of (puppet) Reorganized National Government of China in Japanese occupied regions of China. Former friend of the Yuan family before he turned collaborator.

Yoshiro Kazuki, General; **Kazuki** is surname - Japanese military officer and one of the targets in Yuan Wen-Ying's resistance mission.

Wang Jing-Wei - President of (puppet) Reorganized National Government of China in Japanese occupied regions of China.

Yao Kang - Second highest ranking member of Shanghai branch of Tian Di Hui (honored title "White Paper Fan".)

Yuan Guo-Hui - Yuan Wen-Ying's older brother. (He is referred to but does not appear in story.)

Yu-Lan, Zhang - Member of Tian Di Hui. Daughter of prominent family which supports the collaboration puppet government.

THE MOON CHASER

In one night, Yuan Wen-Ying can take down the Japanese commander who slaughtered masses in Nanking. Can she set the plan in motion if she has to destroy the unrequited love of the only one remaining by her side?

CHAPTER 1

THE DEAD BODY beside the lamp post caught Wen-Ying's eyes and she swerved her bike away from it to the other side of the road. The corpse had been lying there for three days. No one had yet come to remove it.

Not wanting to suffer a closer glimpse, Wen-Ying tucked her chin and looked away. Instinctively, she held her breath until the body was well behind her, even though she was nowhere near enough to catch the sour whiff of decay or contagious disease.

In Shanghai, dead bodies were not an uncommon sight. Victims of gang fights killed on the streets. Beggars plagued by illnesses passing away in the dark hours of the night. Such were the facts of life in the city where she had grown up. The sight of death didn't shock anyone. Back when the Chinese ruled this place, street cleaners would haul the corpses away and dispose of them before dawn. When rush hour rolled in, another bustling day would begin. Business as usual, as Findlay, her old boss at the British consulate would say.

Not so anymore. Since the Japanese invasion in '37, this once prosperous city had become a living hell and nothing was ever usual again. And when Pearl Harbor happened in '41, even the untouchable International Settlement succumbed. Now, another three years later, buses no longer operated. The trams ran only sporadically and most private automobiles ceased to travel the roads. Streetlights and traffic lights stopped working. Public services of every kind had all but disintegrated.

Shanghai today was nothing like what it used to be. Here on Avenue Joffre, mannequins in fancy Chanel dresses no longer gazed elegantly from the storefronts. Bulgari jewelry and Rolex watches no longer shone on display in shop windows. In their place was a dark emptiness. An oppressive, suffocating void that sucked the life out from every corner, lane, and alley. Sometimes, Wen-Ying thought it would smother her and leave her dead on the street next.

She tightened her grip on the handlebars and sped up. For a moment, she almost felt she could escape if only she peddled fast enough. With each rising breath, she quickened her feet.

"Ay, watch the road!" A coolie shouted at her. Wen-Ying gasped and braked to a stop. Lost in her thoughts, she didn't see him dragging his rickshaw up the cross street. She almost hit him.

"Sorry," she said.

The coolie threw her a nasty glare. He opened his mouth, ready to hurl a barrage of insults at her. Before he could, he stomped into a pothole filled with gray water, a discarded cigarette package, and floating concrete debris.

"Motherfucker." He grimaced as he pulled out his foot. His homemade cotton shoe was soaked.

What bad luck. The coolie sure had his lintel turned upside-down today. Hopefully, he wouldn't catch any diseases. Mosquitoes and flies loved the static water in potholes. Who knew what germs were festering in them? The rot-filled potholes, the decomposing corpses, and all the garbage strewn around invited roaches and rats. An epidemic should break out any day now.

Wen-Ying got off her bike and walked on past a line of customers queuing up around the block to buy yams and roots. Scavenging farmers had dug these up from the deserted grounds in the rural countryside to sell in the city. One could hardly find places to buy rice now. But even if luxury food items like rice, meat, and vegetables were available for sale, only the privileged few could afford to buy any. Like the Japanese, their allies, and collaborators.

"Please, I beg you, please, help us a little," said a woman as she clasped her bony hands in prayer to the people standing in line to buy the scarce supply of yams. The baby tied with a *mehdai* to her back wailed as the woman went from one person to the next. Everyone squirmed away as she approached them in her ragged blouse and dirt-smeared pants. Looking dazed and lost, she walked toward Wen-Ying.

Startled, Wen-Ying stepped back. The woman's sunken cheeks and hollowed eyes looked like a skull. The white spots on the woman's greasy hair frightened her even more. Were they dandruff or lice?

Averting her eyes, Wen-Ying veered her bike away. She couldn't help the woman or the hundreds more like her squatting on the sidewalks, too weak and hungry to move. Many of them were refugees who swarmed the International Settlement when the Japanese first invaded the Chinese-controlled parts of the city seven years ago. Too bad for them, the International Settlement provided no safe haven. In the end, the British and Americans who lived here couldn't even save themselves. When the Japanese finally blew up Pearl Harbor four years later, they seized the International Settlement controlled by the British and the Americans too. After that, they rounded up all the foreign citizens of the Allied countries in Shanghai and hauled them off to internment camps. They took away Findlay too. That pompous, racist human scum.

Findlay. How she despised that man. How many times had she heard him demean the Chinese, calling them "sneaky yellow scoundrels," "treacherous snakes," or "slanty-eyed rats." He would say all these things, even in her presence.

It wasn't only what he said. Foreigners like him thought they were superior. They came here, poisoned her people with their opium, and imposed treaties and demands to raid China to build their own wealth. All the same while, they set up their fancy clubs, racetracks, and dancehalls where no Chinese were allowed.

And then they did allow the Chinese into the racetracks. But only when they realized they could rake in more cash from the Chinese addicted to gambling. And only on limited days when they could tolerate the natives' presence.

She huffed at the thought. Those foreigners and their haughty attitudes. She loathed them. Even the ones who showed civility to the Chinese. Their kindness always felt like condescension. She didn't care for their pathetic attempts to make nice. They had no right to claim any part of her country. They should've all just gone away.

The rare hums of a motorcade broke her train of thoughts. Glancing sideways, Wen-Ying saw the line of Japanese military vehicles driving down the street, flaunting their flag with the red circle and stripes symbolizing the rising sun. Pedestrians moved aside and turned their gazes. Any perceived gesture of disrespect toward the Imperial Japanese Army could invite a savage beating, or worse, death.

Wen-Ying tipped her hat lower as the enemy roared past. She doubted those short squashes riding in the Isuzu Type 94s could see her face from that distance. Even if they could see her, those lowly ranked soldiers wouldn't know their superiors were keeping their eyes on her. The IJA command suspected she was a member of Tian Di Hui, the Heaven and Earth Society.

And she was. She'd been part of the secret resistance group since the Japanese established the puppet state of Manchukuo. Her role in Tian Di Hui was the reason why she, Yuan Wen-Ying, daughter of the prominent Yuan family in Shanghai who didn't need to work, took a job as a translator for the British consulate before the war. As she'd told everyone, her reason for working there was to steer business opportunities back to the Chinese. Behind the scenes, she dispatched information on British political and military development to her network. Her English skills and position with the British government made her invaluable to their resistance efforts. Even now, they needed her to transcribe intelligence obtained from secret radio transmissions and liaise with various foreign agents and governments supplying them arms. If those Japanese soldiers knew who she was and captured her, they would torture her until she told them everything she knew.

The army motorcade disappeared down the street. The hulk of an abandoned double-decker bus now remained the only vehicle on the road. What would Findlay think if he saw this? Was he even alive anymore? At internment camps, the Japanese tortured their prisoners. Being a highly-ranked British government official, the Japanese would have done anything to get information out of him. Findlay was more than fifty years old. Even if by miracle they didn't lay their hands on him, she couldn't see how he could stand a chance against the eternal darkness of the cramped and crowded prison cells. How could he survive the stench of human waste never cleaned and the diseases carried by rodents and bugs?

The thought of Findlay suffering gave her no joy. She'd seen the horrifically mangled bodies of Tian Di Hui members when the Japanese released them back from prison. She wouldn't wish that on anyone.

An elderly man came out of the store, passing the queue without looking at anyone. He hugged his bag of yams to his chest like they were precious treasures. Suddenly, one of the beggars squatting on the pavement bolted up. A scrawny teenage boy. His eyes fierce like a wild animal, the boy rammed into the elderly man, knocked him to the ground, and snatched the bag from his chest. The bag tore and the yams fell out. The boy grabbed what he could, biting into a raw yam in his hand as he broke away. Seeing the remaining yams rolling on the ground, the other beggars closest to the scene rushed to snag them away, leaving the fallen old man crying out in pain. Those who were standing in line yelled at the beggars to stop, but none would come to the old man's aid for fear of losing their spot in the queue.

Quickly, Wen-Ying pulled her bike over to the old man. "Are you all right?" she crouched down and asked, all the while keeping one hand on her bike. "Are you hurt?"

"They stole my yams." The old man pointed helplessly at the beggars who had gotten away. Tears streamed down his face. "They stole my yams. There's nothing left. Nothing left. What will I do now? What will my family eat now? I don't have any money left."

Wen-Ying raised her head. No way she could recover the stolen yams anymore. The beggars had scattered. She looked at the line. The yams would likely sell out before everyone could buy. Still, she reached into her pocket and discreetly took out a Mexican silver dollar. "Buy again." She stuck the dollar into his palm.

The old man's tears stopped. He looked at her. "*Xiao jie…*," he said, his mouth falling agape.

"Go buy some more." She gave him an encouraging smile.

"Thank you." The old man's face finally eased. "*Xiao jie*, thank you." He started to get up and Wen-Ying gave his arm a lift.

Holding the coin tightly in his fist, the old man hobbled to the end of the queue. Wen-Ying didn't know if she did a good thing or not. The poor man might be standing in line for another hour, only to end up with empty hands.

She checked her watch and hopped back onto her bike. Whatever would happen to him, she had to leave. It was almost four o'clock. The other Tian Di Hui members were waiting.

CHAPTER 2

WEN-YING RODE her bike along the street into a small alley until she reached a shikumen building hidden away from the main road. At the entrance with a small sign that said, "OFFICE OF DR. WU ZHAN-PENG," she stopped. After chaining her bike to the metal rack, she slung her canvas bag across her shoulder and entered. Inside, she clutched the strap of her bag and took a quick scan of the room. A faint ray of sunlight flowed through the small window, illuminating the phrase COMPASSIONATE HEART, COMPASSIONATE SKILLS written in calligraphy and framed on the wall. The fluorescent tube on the ceiling did little to further brighten the place.

No patient sat on the bench in the dim waiting area. Wen-Ying let out a subtle breath of relief and loosened her hand.

The lone nurse at a desk glanced up.

"How are you?" Wen-Ying gave her a quick smile. "I have an appointment with Dr. Wu," she said as she flashed the Tian Di Hui hand gesture signifying the word *Ming*.

Ming. A common, innocent term with varied meanings: light, clarity, understood, overt. It could even simply be a boy's name. For Tian Di Hui members, however, *Ming* stood for the Ming

Dynasty. It was a reminder of their battle cry, "Rebel against Qing and revive Ming." They had resisted for centuries the foreign Manchurian rulers who established the Qing Dynasty.

But Tian Di Hui wasn't always a group of insurgents plotting subversive activities. During peacetime, its members had taken it upon themselves to help the weak and aid the poor, and to assume the role of vigilante to carry out justice when needed and deserved.

Seeing Wen-Ying's hand signal, the nurse's tired eyes became alert. "You may go in." She pointed to the door to her left.

Keeping a straight face, Wen-Ying opened the door and entered the room. Ignoring the wooden desk, chair, and exam table, she pushed the bookcase concealing a secret entrance to the narrow corridor leading to the back of the house.

In one of the hidden rooms at the end of the corridor, Dr. Wu's wife, Lian jie, was serving everyone bowls of chicken congee. Wen-Ying's stomach grumbled as the savory smell hit her nose.

"Wen-Ying? You've arrived," said the man standing at the head of the long table.

"Fan Da Ge." Wen-Ying took off her hat. Like everyone else, she called him *Da Ge,* the honorific for addressing someone who was the eldest brother. For Tian Di Hui, *Da Ge* was how members addressed their "First Helm", and no one deserved this honor more than Fan Yong-Hao. Despite his youthful age of thirty-five, he had turned Tian Di Hui into the most fearsome resistance group in Shanghai. He pulled off their biggest coup when he assassinated the Japanese-appointed mayor of the occupied sectors of Shanghai in 1940. He'd shot the traitor with his own hand. Fan had led them on countless plots to bomb enemy buildings and supply depots; blow up trains, railroads, and bridges; plant mines on land and in water. He'd wreaked so much havoc, the Japanese had put a price on his head.

For Wen-Ying herself, she didn't mind calling Fan "*Da Ge*" at all. Now that she had no more family around her, her brothers and sisters in Tian Di Hui were the only family she had left. When she pledged her allegiance to the group, she had sworn to accept Heaven as her father and Earth as her mother, and to give their members her unwavering loyalty. If Fan would risk his life over and over again for their cause, then she would too. As long as there was hope to drive out Japan, she would dive into boiling water and ride through seas if Fan asked.

"Do you have any updates?" Fan asked.

"Yes." Wen-Ying took from her bag the latest BBC news reports she had translated and handed it to him. His sure eyes and confident air always made her feel safe and grounded.

Fan flipped through the pages. "Good job," he commended her. "Eh! The Allies liberated Brussels!"

"Yes." Wen-Ying was thrilled too when she first heard the news. The Allies' successful landing at Normandy had given them their first shot of hope. They all wanted to believe that soon the forces on their side would crush their own enemy too.

This was not a hollow hope. The United States was finally on Japan's tail. "I decoded the message from my American contact." She gave Fan a second set of papers. They were messages from Greg Dawson, the American pilot she had met before the war who became one of the Flying Tigers and was now serving with the U.S. Army Air Forces' Twenty-Third Fighter Group. He regularly sent her updates on their progress against the Japanese out in Xinjiang.

Good old Greg Dawson. That simple fella from Kansas couldn't understand that a proper Chinese woman would never consider courtship by a man who was not Chinese. He never took it to heart though when she rejected his advances. As the war intensified, he became one of her most trusted sources for outside information and one of Tian Di Hui's most reliable carriers of ammunition and supplies for their covert operations.

"We'll get the news onto the streets tomorrow," Fan said. The

Shanghai locals had no access to outside news. Even if they could access foreign media, the Chinese wouldn't understand news reported in English. If left to the Japanese propaganda machine, they would believe Japan was winning, and they would lose the will to fight back. To counter Japanese lies, Wen-Ying diligently listened to BBC wireless broadcasts every day, not only to keep the members of the resistance informed, but also to enable them to create their own propaganda leaflets for mass dissemination to the public underground.

"Come," Lian jie gave Wen-Ying a bowl of congee. "Eat some. A patient of Old Wu's brought him a chicken today. We don't know when we'll have another meal with meat again."

Wen-Ying took the bowl. Such generosity. Dr. Wu and Lian jie could've kept the chicken to themselves. The older couple weren't sworn members of Tian Di Hui, and they were taking on huge risks to themselves by providing a cover for the group to meet and plan their next actions.

The other members gathering for the meeting today, Yao Kang, Zhang Yu-Lan, and Huang Jia-Ming, moved to make room for Wen-Ying at the round table. Yao Kang and Huang Jia-Ming were Fan's right and left hands. Yao being their "White Paper Fan," their branch's second in command. Huang ranked third, their "Third Home Guard." Wen-Ying herself was their "Fourth Home Guard," alternately called their "Golden Phoenix."

Wen-Ying took a seat between Yao Kang and Yu-Lan. The hunger pangs were now boring holes in her stomach. Disregarding all care for good manners, Wen-Ying sat down and devoured the soup. It really was a soup more than a congee. The amount of rice used wasn't nearly enough to make a pot of thick porridge to feed more than four people. To compensate, Lian jie boiled the rice to the point where it had turned into a thin paste. As for the chicken, no wonder Lian jie chose to make a congee. The sad foul had hardly any meat. Making it into a dish couldn't have satisfied anyone. Boiling its bones in the congee, on the other hand, gave the meal a mouth-watering flavor and provided them all a rare treat.

Halfway through, Wen-Ying made an effort to slow down. She wanted to make the bowl of congee last. She never thought she would know hunger. Growing up, she had eaten the best cuisines in the world. Shark fins, abalone, prawns and crabs, thousand-years old ginseng. Her mother used to take a cup of sweet swallow's nest soup every night before going to bed.

Savoring every drop, Wen-Ying closed her eyes, remembering a time before the Japanese invaded. Before her life shattered to pieces.

"Delicious?" Zhang Yu-Lan, who was sitting next to her, nudged her by the shoulder.

"Yes," Wen-Ying said. Since she went underground, Yu-Lan had become her best friend. Like herself, Yu-Lan came from a very wealthy and highly respected family. The difference was, Yu-Lan's parents and brothers were still around. They remained well and alive in Shanghai, and retained their status in society, having become collaborators of the Japanese. Her oldest brother held a high-ranking position as Secretary of Transportation with the city's Reorganized National Government. This puppet regime, nominally headed by Wang Jing-Wei, the traitor who defected from the Kuomintang, now governed Shanghai at the whims of the occupying enemy.

Some in Tian Di Hui had doubted her at first, but Yu-Lan had proven herself invaluable. As the daughter of the Zhang family, she could navigate Wang Jing-Wei's circle and eavesdrop on their high officials, even as they overlooked her as nothing more than a young woman of leisure.

"Fan Da Ge, I've got news," Yu-Lan said. She poured Wen-Ying a cup of tea from the pot on the table. "My parents and I had dinner with Zhou Fo-Hai last night." Zhou was the puppet regime's Finance Minister. "He said the IJN Rear-admiral Yamauchi will be attending a private viewing of *Renowned for*

Centuries to Come next Thursday night. Seven o'clock at the Guanglu Grand Theater."

"Really?" Fan turned the teacup in his hand. *Renowned* was an anti-Western movie released last year by Zhonghua Production in collaboration with the Manchukuo Film Association. Shanghainese film makers had made the movie, but both film studios were under Japanese control.

Yu-Lan looked intently at him. "It's a good chance if you want to take him out. A drive-by assassin can catch them off guard."

Fan's lips curled up into a half-smile. They all knew that half-smile meant he intended to do exactly that.

Quietly, Wen-Ying finished the last bit of her congee and licked her lip. Yu-Lan watched her, then glanced at the empty bowl. "Next time, I'll try to bring a box of mooncakes."

Mooncakes. Wen-Ying's mouth watered. The Mid-Autumn Festival was coming up. Traditionally, every family would spend the night eating mooncakes and sipping tea while admiring the full moon. This year, few people would have the luxury of eating mooncakes. People were starving and most would not be in any mood to celebrate.

"Only say that if you can deliver on your promise," Huang teased her. "Or else I can't bear the disappointment."

"Don't pressure her." Yao Kang gave him a disapproving look. "You're always thinking about food. Would you die if you eat a little less?"

Huang twitched his mouth and didn't reply. When Yao Kang looked away, Huang flicked his eyes. Wen-Ying didn't blame him. Yao Kang always picked on him. He told everyone that he was criticizing Huang for his own good, that he was teaching Huang how to properly command those in the lower ranks. Wen-Ying didn't believe him though. Huang was smarter, but he ranked lower because he was five years younger and he joined Tian Di Hui later. Wen-Ying thought Yao Kang felt threatened.

Yu-Lan changed the subject. "I have another useful piece of gossip."

"What's that?" Wen-Ying asked.

"I went with Madam Mei Si-Ping to see a palm reader."

"Mei Si-Ping?" Fan leaned forward. "Wang Jing-Wei's Interior Minister?"

"That's him," Yi-Lan said. "I've been making an effort to get close to his wife. The palm reader told her she needs to watch out for poisonous women out to sabotage her. She was very shaken. After we left, she privately confessed to me. Mei Si-Ping has a mistress. A young sing-song girl. Mei put her up in a luxury flat near the Bund. I know the address. Madam Mei wanted me to advise her whether she should go and confront the girl."

"Huh." Fan crossed his arms.

"She said he had mistresses before, but this one's different. This one's got him spellbound. He's smitten with her."

Huang Jia-Ming snickered, then turned serious. "We can threaten to harm her. We can use her to force him to divulge information to us."

"You're always like a turtle drawing back its head." Yao Kang pointed at Huang. "Why bother threatening with words? Just kidnap her. If we hold her hostage, Mei Si-Ping will have to tell us whatever we want to know or we won't let her go."

"Do we need to go that far?" Huang frowned. "Why frighten the poor girl if we don't need to?"

"So what if she's frightened? She's just a whore."

"Enough," Fan told both of them. "I don't want to rush into anything. We should look into the girl's background first. If she's clever, we might be able to buy her off and make better use of her. If she's dumb, then we'll see."

Yao Kang held his tongue, but huffed out a big breath of air and rolled his eyes at Huang. Actually, Wen-Ying agreed with Huang. Hanging a threat over Mei Si-Ping's head could compel him to answer to them for the long haul. Kidnapping the girl now, when they didn't know what they wanted from Mei, would be shortsighted.

But that was Yao Kang's problem. He had courage in spades, but he lacked wit. Sometimes, Wen-Ying wondered if Huang might be more qualified for the role of the White Paper Fan.

Yao probably wondered about that himself. That might be why he constantly found fault with Huang.

The door to their room opened. "Sorry I'm late," said the young man who walked in. Wen-Ying looked up. Involuntarily, her heart flipped.

"Takeda!" Fan broke into a smile.

"Fan Da Ge," Masao Takeda returned his greeting. His eyes landed next on Wen-Ying. Quickly, Wen-Ying lowered her head and looked away.

"As long as you can come, that's good." Fan invited him to take a seat. "What news do you have?"

Takeda took out a map of the port of the Whangpoo River and laid it on the table. "It's been confirmed. The *Kiyohashi* will arrive at Shanghai tomorrow afternoon at 1500 hours."

Fan crossed his arms and held his fist to his chin. *Kiyohashi* was a freight carrier for the Kwantung, the most formidable military force of the Imperial Japanese Army. In April, the Japanese launched Operation Ichigo, a new offensive to push the lines of their occupied territories in China to seize control of the entire length of the railway from Peking to Hong Kong. A successful expansion deeper into the South would enable them to take over the airfields in the Canton region and link up their forces with those in Saigon and French Indochina. Their effort relied heavily on supplies coming in from the North.

For the last month, Fan had been hatching a plot to blow up the *Kiyohashi* to derail one of the Kwantung's major supply vessels. "The *Kiyohashi* will be docked for three days for the army to unload," said Takeda. "It's scheduled to sail back to Japan on September 5th."

Fan exchanged a glance with Yao Kang and Huang Jia-Ming. Their plan was simple, but dangerous as always. As usual, they would work with *Juntong,* the Chinese secret police, who would supply the bombs. The day when the *Kiyohashi* was scheduled to arrive, operatives of *Juntong* would store backpacks of explosives in a sampan at a nearby dock. At night, Fan would lead Yao Kang and Huang Jia-Ming to blow up the ship. They would carry the backpacks on their bodies, row the sampan out toward the *Kiyohashi,* while a *Juntong* operative served as the lookout. When the sampan came near enough, they would swim out, attach their backpacks to the bottom of the *Kiyohashi* for a time-delayed explosion, and escape back to the sampan before the bombs went off.

"Your plans always terrify me," Yu-Lan said to Fan. "The *Kiyohashi* is bigger than the vessels you've blown up before. Are you sure it's going to work?" She cowered and flashed him a doubtful stare.

Fan didn't even blink. "We'll be fine. My SACO training prepared me for this." SACO was the top-secret operation set up by the U.S. Navy and Dai Li, the head of *Juntong*. Through that arrangement, American naval intelligence units were deployed in rural China to set up weather observation depots and to train Chinese resistance fighters. "The guerrilla tactics the Americans taught me haven't failed me yet."

Listening to the group discuss the details of their plan, Wen-Ying stole a glance at their informant. Masao Takeda joined Tian Di Hui just before Japan invaded the Chinese-controlled parts of Shanghai in 1937. His mother was Chinese. He himself was born in Shanghai and grew up in this city. When he was fourteen, his father passed away from cholera.

Why did he choose to ally with his mother's native land instead of his father's? Wen-Ying had always been curious, but never dared to ask. Every time she saw him, she felt self-conscious. Whenever he came near her, she became clumsy and awkward. She could never speak to him without feeling jittery and ill at ease. All she could do was to keep away from him and try to act normal.

But she had no way of avoiding him totally even if she wanted. Takeda was a key part of their operation. Because his father was Japanese and he spoke their language, he easily convinced the occupying forces his allegiance lay with his paternal roots. The Imperial Japanese Army hired him as a civilian representative to aid and advise Wang Jing-Wei in governing and rebuilding of Shanghai. They wanted him to keep watch over Wang and his people and to make sure they submit to Japanese rule to support a total victory of Japan in the East. What they didn't know, of course, was that Takeda had joined the Japanese occupational forces to serve as the Tian Di Hui's undercover agent and informant.

While Wen-Ying's thoughts wandered, Yao Kang held up the map and squinted. "Which port will the *Kiyohashi* be docking at again?"

Takeda rose from his seat and came around the table. "Here." He pointed at a spot on the map and began explaining the ship's route. His side only inches away from her, Wen-Ying stared away. The warmth of his presence quickened her pulse. Why did he have this effect on her? He'd helped Tian Di Hui a lot, she'd admit that. But so did all the others. Why should his participation move her more than anyone else's?

Besides, however much he was contributing to her cause, it didn't change the fact that he was half Japanese. It was ridiculous how often the thought of him would, from out of nowhere, break into her mind.

She shifted in her seat so she would face away from him. It was all too overwhelming. Takeda distracted her and confused her when she needed to keep a straight head. Best to keep a distance between them. She had too many important tasks at hand.

CHAPTER 3

"LET ME WALK YOU HOME," Takeda offered as Wen-Ying picked up her hat to leave the clinic.

"There's no need. Besides, I came on my bike."

Undeterred, Takeda came closer to her. "I have news for you about your old family home," he whispered under his breath.

Wen-Ying paused. The mention of her old home tore her heart. She hadn't set foot in there since she went underground three years ago. Soon after that, the beautiful villa where she had grown up was taken over by the Japanese and Wang Jing-Wei's new collaborationist regime.

"I'll tell you about it when we're somewhere more private," Takeda said.

Wen-Ying gripped her hat. "All right." She relented. Takeda's eyes lit up but she pretended she didn't notice.

On the street, they walked silently to the small flat where Tian Di Hui had arranged for her to stay this month. These days, she moved around a lot. She never stayed at any one place for long for fear of being tracked. While she wasn't the most wanted person on the occupying forces' list, her name had come up as a radical. The Japanese had people out looking for her. With enemy eyes and ears all around, she had to take extra care to evade their attention.

She pushed her bicycle, fiddling with the handlebars now and then to lighten the awkwardness she felt. Next to her, Takeda strolled along. "How about I walk your bike for you?"

"Not necessary," she said. She needed the bike between them. To keep a distance. "You're wearing a suit. It wouldn't look right for you to be pushing a bike." Without thinking, she turned the handlebars lightly away from him.

If the world was not at war and they had met under different circumstances, would they be walking with each other like this?

Of course not. If she had no official business with him, she wouldn't have become acquainted with him. She was a respectable young woman. Not someone who would casually let a half-Japanese man walk her home.

The whole way, they never said a word. Somehow, while weaving through a group of pedestrians crossing the street, he had walked around the bike to be on her other side. He was walking closer and closer to her. She should move further away. And yet, she couldn't. It was hard enough stopping herself from moving closer to his warmth.

Thankfully, they had arrived. She stopped in front of the wooden door of an old lane house where she was staying.

"We're here." She turned slightly toward him while she took out her keys, feeling too nervous to look him in the eye. He gazed at the front of the building and frowned, but didn't say anything.

Wen-Ying opened the door and pulled the bike inside. The building housed three separate units. A family of six lived in the larger unit on the first floor. She lived in one of the smaller units on the second floor. The third unit, as far as she knew, was empty. She suspected it belonged to Tian Di Hui as well, but didn't see any reason to ask and find out if that was the case. She'd be moving elsewhere in another month's time anyway.

She swung the strap of her canvas bag over her shoulder and lifted the bike to take it upstairs.

"Let me help you." Takeda rushed up to her. "It's heavy."

"I'm fine. I do this every day," she said, keeping her head down as she dragged the bike.

"Let me do it." He scowled and grabbed the bike from her. Easily, he carried it up the steps, a chore for which she usually had to expend the strength of nine oxen and two tigers.

Following him, Wen-Ying gazed up. Her eyes involuntarily drawn to the shape of his back. The back which showed the physique of someone in his prime. He had the force of a man who would take charge. Like someone who would blaze the trail and lead the women and the children to safety if caught in a storm.

What woman would not be drawn to such force?

"Which unit?" Takeda asked and turned around when he reached the top of the stairs.

Her heart jumped. Reflexively, she shifted her eyes away. "The one on the left," she answered and came up beside him. She didn't mean to stare. She hoped he didn't notice.

Keeping her eyes low, she fumbled with her keys, then opened the door. The simply furnished room was a far cry from the luxury villa where she had lived before the war. All this unit had was a single-sized bed, a wooden table that seated two people at most, and a chest of drawers no bigger than two nightstands lined up together. The cold, bare concrete walls reminded her how lonely she felt at times, but at least there was a little balcony. She could stand out there and watch the children from the neighborhood play with crickets in the back alley.

She pulled the little string of the switch to turn on the one light bulb dangling from a cord in the ceiling. The light hardly illuminated the room. Not that it mattered. Curfew would begin in an hour, and lights out would follow soon after.

"Would you like some tea?" Wen-Ying took the canvas bag off her shoulder and dropped it on the bed.

"Yes." Takeda set the bike against the wall and looked around the room. He creased his brows slightly but again didn't say anything.

Wen-Ying unscrewed the top of her thermos and poured hot tea into two cups, then handed one to him. "This low-grade *puer* is all I have."

"Thank you." He accepted the teacup and took a sip, then gazed up and smiled at her. A bright spark lit up his eyes. She dared not look at it directly for fear it might ignite something she could not steer or understand.

"What did you want to tell me about my old home?" She walked away from him to the table.

"I thought you might like to know who they turned your house over to."

"Who?"

"Liu Kun and his wife Shen Yi."

Wen-Ying jerked up her head. Once, Shen Yi was her older brother Yuan Guo-Hui's fiancée. Their parents had arranged for them to marry since before their births when their mothers became pregnant at the same time. That was before Guo-Hui decided he wanted free love and broke off the engagement. Shortly after, Shen Yi married the widower Liu Kun, who was twenty years her senior but whose wealth did not pale comparing to the Yuan family. Other than the fact that Liu Kun took Shen Yi as a *tian fang*, a younger wife to replace one who was deceased, their marriage was a good match. What Wen-Ying couldn't have foreseen was Shen Yi and her husband turning and joining the collaborators.

Such unspeakable betrayal. A treason.

Liu Kun gained favor with the Japanese by becoming their point man in destroying those who fought their enemy occupiers. In the New Asia Hotel, he had a permanently reserved room where he tortured and decapitated Chinese resistance fighters, journalists and reporters, and bankers and businessmen who supported the resistance movement.

And Shen Yi. How could she? Did she know what her husband was doing? Wen-Ying's family had watched Shen Yi grow up. Wen-Ying herself and her parents favored Shen-Yi highly. When Guo-Hui ended the engagement, they had done everything they could to try to change his mind.

Guo-Hui knew better after all.

Takeda dipped his head, then warily glanced up. "I heard, Shen Yi specifically requested your house."

Wen-Ying's jaws clenched. Such a spiteful woman Shen Yi turned out to be. Even now, she could not forgive Guo-Hui. She meant to show the world that one way or another, she would take and possess everything that would have belonged to her had she become Guo-Hui's wife.

Liu Kun had his own reasons for wanting to take over the old Yuan mansion. He'd always blamed her brother for usurping his seat on the Shanghai Municipal Council, the local governing body of what was once the International Settlement of Shanghai, when the sector was still under British and American control.

And now, he would usurp what should belong to Guo-Hui.

"They're moving in tomorrow," Takeda said. "I wanted to let you know so you wouldn't find out about it by surprise."

"Thank you." Wen-Ying put down her cup. This stab in the back struck her to the core. Even if Shen Yi still held a grudge against her brother, did she have no regards for the years of relationship she had with the rest of the Yuan family?

In deep thoughts, Wen-Ying clutched the back of the chair.

"It's almost a full moon tonight." Takeda walked out to the balcony. Wen-Ying blew a deep breath and joined him. "In another three weeks, it'll be the Mid-Autumn Festival." He turned and flashed her a smile.

She looked up at the moon slowly rising above the darkening sky. The Mid-Autumn Festival was a time when farmers celebrated their harvests. It was also a night for mortal folks to revel and catch a glimpse of the Moon Goddess, Chang 'e.

According to legend, Chang 'e lived in an ancient time when the world used to have ten suns. Normally, the ten suns rose in succession. One day, an anomaly happened and all ten suns rose together. Under the sweltering heat, all the plants and trees began to shrivel and all the rivers and lakes began to dry. Soon, the heat would scorch all the farms, and no water would be left to irrigate the crops. The entire population on earth would die.

To save the world, Hou Yi, the husband of Chang 'e famous for his phenomenal archery skills, shot down nine suns so that only one would remain. When the climate of the world was restored, the Queen Mother of Heaven rewarded him by giving him an elixir. If a person drinks half the bottle, he would become immortal. If a person drinks the entire bottle, he would become a god and ascend to Heaven.

Hou Yi hid the elixir at home and planned to share it with his wife so they could live together forever. But one day, while he was out hunting, his apprentice Feng Meng came to his home and demanded Chang 'e turn over the elixir. In fear, Chang 'e took the elixir and fled. While Feng Meng chased after her, she drank the entire bottle to keep it from him. Immediately after she finished, she flew up to the moon and became a goddess. When Hou Yi returned home and discovered what had happened, he tried to chase after her. But because he was mortal, he could never reach her. Whenever he came close, he would only step into his own shadow under the moon.

In the years since, on the night of August the fifteenth of the lunar calendar when the moon becomes its roundest and brightest, people would gather at night to celebrate the Mid-Autumn Festival and search for Chang 'e in the moon. They say that if you look carefully, you can see her shape in the gray clouds weaving over the moon. If you look even closer, you can see the white jade rabbit that has become her pet too.

Gazing up at the sky, Takeda spread his elbows on the rim of the concrete enclosure. "When I was little, I always had the best lantern for the Mid-Autumn Festival."

Wen-Ying smiled. Children carrying toy-sized paper lanterns to stroll the streets was a Mid-Autumn tradition, along with snacking on mooncakes while drinking tea and admiring the moon.

"My lanterns were always one of a kind," Takeda said. The look of happy memories glowed on his face. "My father would make one for me himself every year. Each year, he would paint a different Japanese animal spirit on it."

"What made him decide to come to China?" Wen-Ying asked.

"He was an orphan. When he was fifteen, he started working at a ramen noodle house. The chef took a liking to him and took him as an apprentice. A wealthy Chinese man came to eat one day while he was visiting Tokyo. He loved the noodles so much, he wanted to partner with the ramen chef to open a new shop in China. The chef ran a successful business already. He had no desire to uproot his family to go to another country, so he suggested the man take my father instead. My father had no money or family. He couldn't have opened a ramen house on his own, so he said yes. One night, the chef let my father prepare the noodles, all the ingredients, and the broth so the Chinese man could taste the ramen my father made and decide if my father's skills met his standard. He liked what my father made. From there on, my father embarked on a new life."

Wen-Ying leaned forward against the wall of the enclosure as she listened. A ramen house. If it weren't for the war, she and Takeda would never have crossed paths. They came from such entirely different social strata. "Did your father find it difficult to live in China?"

"Maybe. He had to learn to speak a new language and new ways of doing things. I don't think he thought of his experience that way though. He was very happy here. His ramen house in China was a huge success. And then, he met my mother."

"Oh?" Wen-Ying glanced sideways at him. Now she was curious. It would be shocking today for a Chinese woman to marry a foreign man, let alone a Chinese woman from a generation before her. How did his mother end up marrying someone from the Eastern Ocean?

"My mother's family sold her when she was three. The family that bought her ran a small shop selling *baozi*. When she grew old enough, she worked at the shop to help out. My father used to go there to get his breakfast. He loved the way they made those steamed pork buns." Takeda chuckled. "Now that I think about it, I'm not sure if the pork buns were really that delicious, or if he just thought they were because my mother was there."

Wen-Ying laughed. His parents were so lucky to have lived at a time when life was more innocent. "What happened then?"

"My mother was getting to be of marriageable age. Since she was bought mainly to be an extra help for her adoptive family, she didn't have any dowry and her prospects weren't very good. My father made his proposal to her family. He saved money for a whole year so he could give the family a monetary gift big enough to marry her."

"And your mother was happy with the arrangement?"

"I think so. I think she knew no man would love and care for her as much as my father."

Wen-Ying relaxed her shoulders. "He sounds like a very unusual man." Nothing like the chauvinists Japanese men were reputed to be.

Takeda smiled. "He told me when he and my mother got married, they still couldn't hold a full conversation. He worked very hard to learn Chinese. She never learned any Japanese except a few words from him here and there. She couldn't even read Chinese. She never went to school. So it was all on him to learn to talk to her."

"They could get along like that?" Wen-Ying asked. Such an extraordinary story. Hard to believe this happened to an illiterate girl who had been sold by her family and an orphan boy.

"Somehow, they managed. They had fifteen happy years together until he died," Takeda said. A trace of sadness tinted his voice.

She knew how he felt. The pain of losing one's parent. "My family used to always watch the moon together in our garden on the night of the Mid-Autumn Festival. In the days leading up to the holiday, our house would be so busy. The houseboys would be preparing boxes of mooncakes to send to all our family friends and my father's clients and business associates. The maidservants would be busy buying food and preparing a big meal. My little sister, Mei Mei, and I would beg our mother to let us help the cook. Of course, we were useless as helpers. We just wanted to play with the dough he used to make fried sesame balls and pastries. Mei Mei liked to use it to make white jade rabbits. Sometimes they actually resembled rabbits. But then the cook would fry them in the pot of oil along with his pastries. When he was done, the rabbits would look like blobs." She stopped. Talking about Mei Mei, she felt a sharp streak of pain, like a sword driving through her heart.

Takeda turned toward her. His tender warmth gave her comfort she hadn't felt since her whole family fell apart.

"Mei Mei had a balcony in her room too." Wen-Ying swallowed back the lump in her throat. "Bigger than this one, of course. A large cypress tree grew beside the wall of our house. It was taller than our roof and some of the branches reached all the way into her balcony. When we were children, we used to ask my father if that tree was the tallest tree in the world. He told us yes and we believed him. On the nights of the Mid-Autumn Festival, when Mei Mei and I grew tired of the talks of the adults in the garden, we would go up to her balcony to try to get closer to the moon. We imagined that if we climbed to the top of that tree, we would reach the moon to find Chang 'e."

"You must really miss her."

"Yes." The image of Mei Mei returned to her mind and prompted her to smile despite her pain. "She was beautiful. It's not my biased opinion either. Everybody praised her and said she was the most beautiful girl in Shanghai."

"You're beautiful," he said. His low voice stirred her, like a hidden fire not yet visible to the eye but whose heat was slowly rising and seeping into their sphere.

"No," she said, avoiding his gaze and keeping her eyes straight at the view ahead. "I can pass for ordinary beautiful if I put on makeup and a pretty dress." These things she didn't do anymore. The part of her life when she used to visit beauty parlors, tailors, and jewelry stores felt like a lifetime ago. She could barely recognize it. "Mei Mei's beauty was ethereal."

"If you say so." He shrugged. "I've never met her, so I wouldn't know." He moved a step closer. "To me, you're beautiful. I remember the first time I saw you. I'd already heard about you. The people in Tian Di Hui, they said there was a young woman, Yuan Wen-Ying. We couldn't have infiltrated the British consulate without her. Back then, everyone still hoped the British would intervene to fend off Japan, given the high financial stake the Britons had in this city."

The British. Wen-Ying sneered as she thought of the Union Jack they used to show off outside the buildings on the Bund. She could never forgive them for bringing that poison, opium, into China and using their military prowess to force China to give up their land. Nor would she ever forget how they stepped all over the Chinese while parading their power as colonial lords. And then, when the threat of war was at the door, they abandoned the Chinese to suffer and fled.

The Japanese who replaced them were even worse. Under

Japanese occupation, thousands upon thousands had been raped, tortured, or murdered.

She detested foreigners. She would never trust them. Never.

"Anyhow," Takeda's voice broke her thoughts, "what I understood was, Yuan Wen-Ying was a key member. Someone indispensable who Tian Di Hui held in high regard."

Her heartbeats quickening, she turned her head away from him.

"That day at the Dragon Boat race, everyone went to cheer for Tian Di Hui's team. They said you would be there too, and I kept looking out to see who was this girl everyone kept talking about. Then I saw you. Standing by the wharf, cheering for our team along with the others. The moment I laid my eyes on you, I knew there was only one thing that would complete my life. I saw you joking and laughing with your girlfriends, and all I wanted was to catch the sound of your laughter. I didn't know until then this kind of feeling was possible. All I've ever wanted since then was you."

Squeezing her arms against her side, she raised her hands to her heart. "You...You can't say these kinds of things to me."

"Why not?" He moved closer beside her. "After everything we've been through, after all the things we've lost, why can't I say what I really feel?"

She dropped her arms and grasped the edge of the enclosure. "I don't believe you. I don't believe a word you said." She pushed her hands against the concrete. "I still don't even know if we should totally trust you. You could be enjoying riches and rewards working for Japan. It makes no sense for you to take the hard road with us." She squared her shoulders and lifted her chin. "Maybe you're playing us all along."

"You don't trust me? After everything I've done?"

"You're Japanese." She glared at him, finally daring to look him in the eye.

"I'm Chinese too." He grabbed her hand and held it up.

"You're lying. Of course you trust me, or else you wouldn't be alone with me here now. You're just telling yourself you don't trust me as an excuse to push me away. The one you really don't trust is yourself. You're afraid you'll find out you feel the same way about me if you let me come closer to you."

Silently, she shook her head. Confusion clouded her mind. A Japanese man? The enemy's blood ran inside him through his veins. No. She couldn't. She wouldn't.

"What would you have me do? I can't split myself in half." He clenched his fist around her hand. For a moment, they stared at each other. Her breaths shortened. The darkened sky hid them from the neighbors' view, but the moonlight shone on his face and she could see the raw emotions agonizing his soul.

"It's late," she said. "You should go."

He frowned in frustration, then loosened his grip. She jerked her hand back and walked to the door. "Be careful walking home." She opened the lock and turned the knob. As he walked out, he looked longingly at her once more. "I'll always be waiting for you."

She watched him turn away and go down the stairs, then closed and locked the door. Alone in her room, she could finally breathe easy again. She leaned back against the door and slumped. Her heart still recovering from the edge of a cliff she had never wanted to climb.

What would she have him do?

What would he have her do? Marry him? Adopt his Japanese last name and identify herself as Madam Takeda? Have children whose paternal allegiance would always be with the land of the rising sun? Her parents' eyes wouldn't close even in their deaths.

She stared across the room at the cup Takeda had left on the small table. It sat there, like a part of him that refused to leave. She walked over to the table and stroked her finger around the side of the cup. She couldn't tell him that the first time she saw him, she felt something stirring within her. An instinctive urge that she could neither control nor explain. She didn't know who he was back then. She only knew she wanted him to come to her, and all the space and distance between them to disappear.

Since then, that urge had only grown stronger. She noticed his every move and heard every echo of his voice. When he stood next to her, she could feel his every breath and every heartbeat.

Why did he have to be part Japanese? After all that had happened in the last seven years, a rift of enmity as deep as a sea of blood had torn open between China and Japan. No matter how much Takeda would do for them to redeem for what his fatherland had done, she could never give herself over to him.

She left the table and took her sleepwear out of the chest of drawers. Methodically, she poured water into the wash basin to wash her face and prepare for bed. The loud shouts of the *Kempeitai*, the Japanese military police, came in through the window from the street and fouled the silence of the night. She tugged the string of the lightbulb and turned out the light.

Pointless. She pulled her pillow lower against her head and curled her body under the thin, coarse blanket. Thinking about Takeda was pointless. With the occupiers still running the city and the war still raging, they had enough problems to think about already. She should put aside the unsolvable question of her and Takeda, and focus on how to drive out the enemy instead.

CHAPTER 4

ACROSS THE STREET from the villa that once belonged to her family, Wen-Ying stood beside a lamp post and watched another truck pull into the driveway behind the one already parked in front of the main entrance. Movers circulated about, unloading trunks and furniture to carry inside. A middle-aged man, whom she gathered must be the head houseboy from the look of his *tangzhuan* uniform, came out of the mansion. Waving his arm wildly, he shouted orders to the group of shirtless laborers tying ropes to a huge, custom-made bed to pull it up to the large porch on the second floor.

Seeing all these strangers roaming about the property, her heart ached. None of them belonged here. And what happened to all her family's furniture? Did any of it still remain inside? No doubt, looters had taken all the most valuable pieces, including her father's antique collection and paintings. If the looters hadn't taken them, surely the Japanese who came afterward had.

What did looters do with antiques and art in times of war? Sell them to the occupiers and collaborators? Probably. She winced at the thought of these vermin's hands touching the things her family owned. Was it not enough that they raped, maimed, and killed their people, took their land, and destroyed their lives? Did they have to contaminate and violate their memories too?

How she missed this place. Growing up, she and her brother and sister had run around this garden playing tag. In the summertime, peonies, camellia, and azaleas would blossom everywhere. She could still see herself and her sister trying to outdo each other jumping ropes, and her brother teasing her for losing to him again in a game of badminton.

"Wah!" A chorus of men cried out from above and below the second-floor porch. The movers lifting the large bed had lost their grip of the ropes and the bed fell several feet before they quickly halted its drop. Wen-Ying wished it had in fact dropped all the way to the ground and smashed to pieces.

"Higher, higher on the left," shouted the mover who appeared to be in charge. His voice carried all the way to where she stood.

She turned her eyes to the other end of the house at the balcony of the room that once belonged to Mei Mei. The flower pots that lined the balustrade were all gone, but the cypress tree beside the balcony still stood, like the last lone guardian of the shadow of the Yuan family's glory days.

The shout of a boy, perhaps thirteen, brought her attention to the side of the street. "Hey! You haven't paid!" The boy ran after two Japanese soldiers. He and his father were selling ceramic bowls and plates out of a cart. The two Japanese shorties, low-level privates with one yellow star on their uniforms, were checking out the goods. While the father wasn't looking, the shorties had taken some of the bowls.

"You haven't paid," shouted the boy as he chased the thieves.

No!

Wen-Ying slapped her hand over her mouth. The boy's father ran after him, but it was too late. Whack! One of the shorties smacked the boy across the face. The other gave him a good slap across the other side, then pushed him down hard. The boy bit back tears and tried to get up. His father rushed to hold him down while he kneeled and shook his hands up and down in prayer to the thieves. One of the Japanese dogs kicked him until he fell, while the other returned to the cart. With one lift, he turned it over. All the bowls and plates fell shattering to the ground.

A hard, sour lump swelled in Wen-Ying's throat. Amidst the thieves' laughter, a shiny black limousine drove by. Without slowing down for the passengers inside to even take note of the scene, it pulled up to the driveway of the mansion. The driver parked, opened the door to the back passengers' seat, and bowed. Shen Yi, bedecked in jewelry in her red embroidered white silk cheongsam, exited the vehicle. Against her better judgment, Wen-Ying stepped closer to try to catch a glimpse of this woman who had come this close to being her sister-in-law.

Was Shen Yi happy now? Did she go to sleep at night relishing the thought that the Yuan family she knew since birth was broken, and all the vestiges that remained of it belonged only to her?

The head houseboy came running to greet her, bowing several times as she ignored him and strutted to the center of the garden to take a sweeping view of her new home. A proud, victorious smile spread across her face.

Standing behind an abandoned cart, Wen-Ying squeezed her fists.

I'm sorry, she said silently to her parents and her grandparents who had built this villa in the hope that it would be passed on for generations. *I failed you. I can't protect what you've left behind. I'm sorry.* She said in her heart over and over again, hoping they could hear her in the next realm.

The wail of the warning siren swelled around her.

Boom!

A loud explosion shook the street. Immediately, another one followed. And another one. American planes had flown into

Shanghai airspace again. Those B-29s, so swift and formidable, had come undetected through the sky to deliver their deadly bombs. With each blast, buildings trembled. Windows cracked and shards of glass flew.

At the villa, men raced to save Shen Yi, surrounding her and scurrying her inside. Workers and movers darted away. Quickly, Wen-Ying dashed back across the street. The sirens split her ears and the ground beneath her quaked. People on the street, already nervous and tense, screamed and ran in chaos, seeking shelters.

Covering her ears with her hands, Wen-Ying huddled in the doorway of a locked, unoccupied shop. Up in the sky, white trails left by the plane lingered. As the sirens continued to shriek and the booms of explosions raged, she wondered if one of the American planes couldn't drop a bomb onto the villa with Shen Yi inside. Memories, treasures, traitors, and pain. Let them all go up in flames. Let everything turn to rubble and nothing of the Yuans could be taken away by anyone again.

CHAPTER 5

WHEN THE SIRENS STOPPED, Wen-Ying picked herself up. Leaving the panicking crowd, she walked back to the safe house. Along the way, she stopped at the black market and picked up a loaf of bread. At least she still had money. She was luckier than most that way. The gold bars her brother Guo-Hui had made her take when they departed their home had carried her along.

Back in her room, she ate her dinner of dry bread and water. After that, all she could do was wait. Takeda had said during their meeting yesterday that the *Kiyohashi* would dock at three o'clock. That was three hours ago. Tonight, Fan Da Ge would try to blow up that ship.

The hour of curfew arrived and the city went dark. In her bed, Wen-Ying counted the hours, unable to sleep. At 2:00 a.m., loud booms of distant explosions shook the city from the direction of the Whangpoo River and she knew Fan's plan to blow up the *Kiyohashi* had gone off. She jumped to her balcony and watched. From the direction of the river, fiery sparks of red and yellow lights pelted to the sky. For more than half an hour thereafter, shouts, sirens, and whistles of the *Kempeitai* howled and shrieked all over the streets. From all the sounds of it, Fan had brought serious damages, if not total destruction, to the Japanese commercial ship.

Her job would be next. As soon as the first silver lining of the sun spread, she hopped on her bike and left for Dr. Wu's office. Once she confirmed whether the plot had succeeded or failed, she would transmit to Dai Li a coded message by radio to give him a short, immediate update.

The streets this morning felt even emptier than usual. A nervous silence hung in the air, interrupted only by the chirps of birds and the shuffles of her bike. Security would be tightened today for sure.

She arrived at the clinic without incident. Just when she was about to take a breath of relief, the haunted look on the nurse's face took her aback.

"Fan Yong-Hao got injured," the nurse said, rubbing away a tear from her eye.

"Injured?" Wen-Ying asked. The words didn't sink in right away. Fan couldn't be injured. The others maybe. But Fan? "How bad?"

"I don't know. He's back there." She pointed to the door of the room with the hidden entrance. "Dr. Wu's trying to save him."

Forcing herself not to panic, Wen-Ying glared at the nurse with a finger over her lip. The nurse immediately closed her mouth, although fear still besieged her eyes. Wen-Ying gave her another firm look to warn her, then opened the door to find the concealed entrance.

In the smaller hidden back room used for tending those injured in their plots, Fan lay on a bed while Dr. Wu pulled a blanket over his body. Dr. Wu's wife, Lian jie, took a wet towel and padded Fan's forehead.

"What happened?" Wen-Ying asked Yao Kang and Huang Jia-Ming. Yao Kang stood scowling and didn't answer. Huang looked up from his chair, his hands still clasped over his knee. "We thought we made it. We swam out from the sampan in the dark. Just swimming in the dark toward the *Kiyohashi*. No one noticed us. Under water, we couldn't even see anything and we followed the directions of the lights of the ships. We planted the bomb to the bottom of the hull, and then we swam away. We thought we'd set the time delay long enough for us to reach the sampan in time." He stopped. His voice cracked as his face scrunched and he dropped his head deeper.

"Go on," said Wen-Ying. A chill rose inside her, spreading from her back to her arms.

"One of the bombs must have gone off early," Huang Jia-Ming said. "That or we swam off course, or maybe the current pushed us harder than we realized. Everything was so dark, it was hard to tell. When we heard the first explosion, we were still swimming. That was when I started swimming in a frenzy. I never swam so fast in my life. I got to the sampan first. Yao Kang got in soon after me. We saw Fan Da Ge swimming toward us and we thought we'd made it. But when we pulled him into the sampan, he was pressing his hand against his waist. Some shrapnel hit him. He told us he was fine. Then he fell unconscious."

Wen-Ying gasped. Trembling, she raised her fist to her mouth.

"At first, we didn't notice how badly he was bleeding. We were soaked. Our lookout rowed the sampan back to the dock and we were supposed to hide inside until morning. But Fan Da Ge started shivering. We debated for a while what to do, and then we decided to take a chance. We stole a rickshaw and brought him back here. Luckily, no one caught us. The explosions distracted everyone and all the *Kempeitai* were rushing to the scene."

"The shrapnel shifted to his vein," said Dr. Wu. "It probably happened when he was swimming."

No. Wen-Ying shuddered. This couldn't be happening. "How is he now?" she cried out. "Will he be all right?"

His head still down, Dr. Wu put his surgical equipment away. "He lost too much blood. There's nothing more I can do."

Wen-Ying took a shaky step toward the bed. Suddenly, her entire center felt empty. She came closer to Fan. His lips looked so white. His face was ghostly pale. For the first time, he looked mortal, not the invincible fighter who could wage a hundred battles for a hundred wins.

Tentatively, she reached out and touched him on the arm. "Fan Da Ge," she whispered. She could feel his body trembling beneath her hand. She watched his chest rise and fall weakly in rhythm with his faint breaths until he drew one final breath. And then, everything stopped. "Fan Da Ge!"

Yao Kang and Huang bolted up and came around him. "Fan Da Ge!" they both called out to him. But it was no use. Fan couldn't hear them anymore.

Wen-Ying shook him with both hands. "Fan Da Ge!" she cried, but he would not respond. His eyes remained closed. She let go of his arm. Her head began to spin and her body felt cold. She gasped for air, unable to breathe. Her arms and legs weakened, and everything around her went dark.

CHAPTER 6

SLOWLY, Wen-Ying opened her eyes to the barren walls of her room in the safe house. What happened? Why was she lying in bed?

"You're awake?" asked Zhang Yu-Lan, who was sitting by her bed.

Wen-Ying pushed herself up from under the cover. A splitting pain throbbed in her head. "How did I get back here?"

"You fainted." Yu-Lan stood up. She wetted a towel from the wash basin and handed it to Wen-Ying. "Lian jie and I brought you back here in a rickshaw. Dr. Wu asked me to look after you until you wake up."

Wen-Ying fell back and put the wet towel over her eyes and forehead. Her headache subsided slightly.

"Here, drink some water." Yu-Lan handed her a full glass.

Her mind still groggy, Wen-Ying took a sip. And then, her memory returned. "Fan Da Ge!" She sat up and swung her legs off the bed. "How's Fan Da Ge?"

Yu-Lan turned away her gaze. When she blinked, tears fell down from her eyes.

"I don't believe it." Wen-Ying lowered her glass and slumped.

"I don't believe it," she said again, as if she could defy the truth if she denied it.

A knock came on the door. Yu-Lan wiped away her tears with the back of her hands and went to see who it was. "Takeda," she said over her shoulder, then opened the door and let him in.

"Wen-Ying." He hurried up to the bed. "Are you all right?"

All right? Was she all right? How could she be all right? They lost Fan Yong-Hao.

"She fainted," Yu-Lan said. "She's fine now. Good thing you came, Takeda. I have to get back home. Will you make sure she regains her bearing?"

"Of course," Takeda sat down next to Wen-Ying by her bed.

"I'm sorry I have to leave," Yu-Lan said to Wen-Ying. "I ought to get home before my parents wonder why I've been gone for so long. You get some rest."

Not wanting to make things difficult for Yu-Lan, Wen-Ying nodded. After she left, Wen-Ying got up.

"Wen-Ying?" Takeda asked.

She ignored him. At the table, she sat down and opened her radio. After turning on the switch, she began entering the message: "The sun came down the mountain. A shooting star flew across the sky." As she transmitted the message, a wall of tears blurred her eyes.

"Wen-Ying." Takeda came up to her.

"Why?" she cried. "Why do all the good people die but all the bad ones live so well? Fan Da Ge, how could he leave us behind like this?"

Takeda turned his head and looked away.

"Fan Da Ge's gone. What will we do now?" Wen-Ying stood up. "What will happen to us?"

"We'll make some adjustments, of course. We'll adapt. We'll—"

She didn't let him finish. "It's been nine years. I've been with Tian Di Hui for nine years. Nine years I've given my life to the cause. I keep hoping we could drive out the Japanese, but the Japanese keep growing stronger. I watch our country's leaders flee in retreat. I stifle my conscience and take directions from that cold-blooded animal Dai Li, knowing all too well he murdered everyone who stood in his way without a blink of an eye. So many times, I felt I lost hope."

She walked over to the entrance to the balcony and gazed up at the sky. "I asked Heaven, what difference does it make if I continue what I do or not? The Japanese will win. We can't defeat them. They have more planes, more ships, more guns. Everything they have to fight with is better. In the end, we will surrender and give up. Fan Da Ge was the only one who kept me believing. With him here, I believe we can fight a good fight. He's all I have to rely on to believe we have hope, because he told us there's hope. Win or lose, I'd follow him to the end. Now he's gone."

She turned around, tears flooded down her face. "Now he's gone, what more can I look to so I can continue to believe? What do I have to hold on to? Where else can I put my hope?"

"You have me!" Takeda pulled her into his arms. "You still have me. You can believe in me."

"You?" She let her weakened body fall against his. The sound of his heartbeat beckoning her as she tried to breathe between sobs.

"I'm here. I'm not going to give up. We won't surrender. Believe me. The Japanese troops can't keep up. Their supplies are depleted. Their casualties are mounting. We still have hope. We do."

She raised her hand and held it against his body. She wanted to feel him closer against her. She wanted someone to hold on to. Someone who could assure her that all the deaths and devastations would be avenged, and all their efforts and losses would be worth it.

"Do you know why I can't give up?" Takeda asked. "It's because of you. You said you could keep going because you believed in Fan Da Ge. Do you know, I can keep going only because I can think of you. There were times I thought I would go crazy myself when I had to stand aside and watch the Japanese soldiers abuse their powers and terrorize people. You don't like taking directions from Dai Li. I don't like taking directions from the Japanese generals either. When I hear about the brutal ways they're torturing the prisoners at the Bridge House, or when I found out they're conducting human experiments up in Harbin, I have to act like I don't care. Every day, I have to act like I feel nothing for anyone they harm. In reality, I just want to run away. I think I would go insane being around these people. I'm afraid if I'm with them long enough, I might lose my own humanity. Sometimes, I lose hope. How can the world have any future when mankind can be this evil?"

Wen-Ying listened in silence. All this time, she'd been avoiding him, never considering how he, too, was a living, breathing person with his own pains. Never giving a thought to what he had to endure. And now, when her world had fallen to its darkest time, he'd reached out a hand and caught her, keeping her afloat.

He wrapped his arms tightly around her. His warm breath blowing next to the skin of her neck. "I can only continue and do what I do if I can think of something in this world I want to save. And that is you."

"Takeda."

"Zheng-Xiong"

"What?"

"Zheng-Xiong. My first name, Masao. In kanji, it's Zheng-Xiong. My parents chose it because it's both a Chinese name and a Japanese name. I know you despise the Japanese part of me. I want you to call me by my name in Chinese."

Masao. Idiot. It broke her heart to hear him say that. "I don't despise you," she whispered.

"Tell me again?"

Her face burning, she said, "I don't despise you. Zheng-Xiong."

He smiled and pulled her hand to his lips.

Enough, she thought to herself. She had insisted on seeing the world through racial lines long enough. She had pushed him away long enough and denied her own feelings for him long enough. Zheng-Xiong. Masao. What did it matter? So what if he had Japanese blood running through him? It wasn't something he could control. What mattered was that he had a heart, and he was by her side.

"We'll go on," he told her. "What Fan Yong-Hao started, we'll finish. We'll keep striking out until the Japanese army crumbles. Fan's spirit in Heaven will look out for us. Do you believe me?"

"I believe you," she said, caressing her cheek against his shoulder.

"Evil can't win against good. We will win. Heaven will be on our side." He looked up and squeezed her hand. "Can you think of the day when there's no more war? We'll be able to leave all these travesties behind. And then, you and I..."

Not hearing anything more from him, she pulled a little away and gazed at his face. "You and I what?"

He dropped his mouth, then blurted, "You and I can open a ramen noodle house."

A ramen house? Wen-Ying laughed through her tears. In that moment, she even felt joy. She just realized, she hadn't laughed in a very long time.

He wiped her tears off her cheek. "From now on, when we're alone, I want you to call me by my Chinese name. Will you do that?"

"Yes." She wrapped her arms around him. "I'll do that, Zheng-Xiong."

CHAPTER 7

IN THE HIDDEN BACK room behind Dr. Wu's clinic, Wen Ying stood beside the empty bed where Fan Yong-Hao took his last breath. Today was the first time she had returned since he passed away.

Fan Da Ge, rest in peace, she said silently to him. *We won't let you down. We'll continue fighting the Japanese. We'll win our country back for sure.*

"Wen-Ying." Yao Kang stepped in. "You're here."

Wen-Ying didn't answer. She kept her stare at the empty bed.

Yao Kang sighed and came next to her. "Fan Da Ge left us so soon. We're all inconsolable."

Wen-Ying touched the top of the blanket. She wanted to bring him back. She didn't know all the pain of losing Fan would flood back like a giant wave when she entered the clinic again. She almost wished she never had to revisit this place.

Not that she had a choice. Today's meeting was called by Dai Li himself. Dai Li rarely appeared in person unless the situation was critical. "Do you know why we were summoned here today?" she asked.

"No," Yao Kang said. "My guess is, maybe Dai Li wants to

discuss who will take over as the leader of Tian Di Hui."

Take over as the leader? Wen-Ying frowned. She didn't want to think about anyone replacing Fan. Anyway, how could they even be talking about this already? Fan's body had barely been laid to rest. He was still their First Helm.

Yao Kang raised his knuckle over his mouth and cleared his throat. "I know no one can take Fan Da Ge's place in everyone's heart," he muttered.

An alert went off in Wen-Ying's head. Why was Yao Kang speaking in such an odd, low voice?

"I would never presume to think I can do anything as well as Fan Da Ge," Yao Kang continued. "But I also know that he would not want our group of brothers and sisters to flounder. He would want us to unite in spirit, and he would want to protect us from harm while we continue our work."

Keeping her expression unchanged, Wen-Ying stood still.

"It's a burden, but I am the White Paper Fan. I'm willing to do Fan Da Ge's work in his stead." Yao stared at her. A glint of hunger sparked in his eyes. Hunger that made her think of a lurking tiger within feet of its prey.

"The subject of our next leader is bound to come up. At that time, you will support me, won't you?" His eyes bore into her.

Was this what Yao Kang cared about right now? Such a shame. Fan had always treated him like a real brother. She dropped her gaze and straightened the corner of the blanket. "It's too early to talk about this, don't you think?"

"You're right." Yao Kang loosened his expression and dropped his shoulders. "To tell you the truth, I don't want to think about such things yet either. The problem is, Dai Li's on his way. I don't think he'll allow the resistance in Shanghai to operate without a helm. He doesn't know Tian Di Hui's inner dynamics the way we do. If he advocates the wrong person, our missions will be at risk. Our lives will be at risk. So we have no choice but to think about this now, even if we're still mourning Fan Da Ge."

Wen-Ying walked away from him and the bed to the center of the room. What Yao Kang said made sense. It was the dark tone beneath his words that troubled her. She raised her eyes again and took a good look at his face. The thirst for power. The desire to be the one at the top. He could barely hide it.

Fan never looked like that. For Fan, power was only something he wielded, not something he wanted.

Yao Kang came beside her. "You're someone who cares greatly about the big picture too. When the time arrives, you'll know to support me, won't you? For the good of Tian Di Hui?"

Would she support him? She couldn't even get used to the idea Fan was dead. Why would she have thought about who should take his place?

But Fan was dead now. And they would need a new leader. Could Yao Kang step up to the job?

The thought gave her doubt. Yao Kang wanted it too much. The phoniness in his voice when he talked about his concern for Tian Di Hui's future made her wary. She didn't like the way he was trying to coax her into supporting him either.

She couldn't deny his contributions to their efforts though. He, too, had risked his life many times when executing their missions. No one could argue his loyalty to their cause.

Not wanting to commit one way or another, she bowed her head. "We should wait to hear what the Tian Di Hui elders have to say first. My support is inconsequential."

"You're too modest," Yao said. "In Shanghai, you're the Golden Phoenix. Your words carry weight. Anyway, we all care about each other like brothers and sisters. At this time, we have to support each other. I'm counting on you."

Not wanting to face him, Wen-Ying kept her stare on the floor. Luckily, Lian jie interrupted them. "What are you two still doing here? Come into the meeting room. General Dai will be here soon."

"Yes, Lian jie." Yao gave Wen-Ying a side glance, then put his hands into his pockets and headed to the meeting room next door. Wen-Ying let out a deep breath and followed him.

In the meeting room, Huang Jia-Ming, Fan's other trusted hand, was already waiting, as were Zhang Yu-Lan and Takeda. When Wen-Ying walked in, Takeda's eyes lit up. Discreetly, he held her gaze.

Zheng-Xiong, Wen-Ying thought and smiled to herself. A tender warmth rose up her heart.

"Wen-Ying." Yu-Lan grabbed her hand. Unlike Yao Kang, Yu-Lan's voice still quivered with sadness. Wen-Ying turned toward Huang. She was about to ask him how he was holding up when she noticed he and Yao Kang had locked eyes. Their demeanors not exactly friendly.

Before she could read the situation, Dr. Wu brought Dai Li into the room. A man with round cheeks and average height followed behind them. Wen-Ying gave the man a quick once over. The only thing distinct about him was how indistinct he appeared. With his passive eyes, unkempt hair, and forgettable face, he looked like any other middle-age laborer or tradesman on the streets.

That, of course, made him a perfect recruit for Dai Li, provided he could be trusted. A perfect agent was one who could pass through the crowd and draw no attention to himself.

With a conciliatory grin, Yao Kang stepped up. "General Dai."

Dai Li held up his hand to stop him. Dr. Wu withdrew from the room and closed the door. Naturally, Dai Li took the spot at the head of the table.

Wen-Ying turned her head and looked away. That spot belonged to Fan. She didn't like seeing someone else there, much less someone like Dai Li.

Yao Kang didn't seem bothered. He came to the side of the table. The rest of them followed. Dai Li acknowledged each of them with a cold, emotionless glance. The indistinct-looking man he brought with him stood humbly behind him.

When Dai Li's glance landed on her, Wen-Ying stood still and stared right back. She wasn't afraid of the man. She didn't work for him. She took directions from him out of respect for the Tian Di Hui elders with whom he had ties, and also because they needed his wide network and resources to fight the Japanese. But she wasn't his agent or his running dog. With a cold-blooded animal like Dai Li, she wanted to make her position clear.

Make it clear not just to him, but also to herself. Unlike him, she still had a conscience. Whatever she might have to do to achieve their end, and however much she had to make deals with the likes of Dai Li, she would not lose sight of the things that were most important.

At the head of the table, Dai Li began to speak. "Fan Yong-Hao passed away at his prime. I feel the deep loss too." He paused to let the words sink in. "Nonetheless, we must continue what we need to do. There is no time to mourn, as a new situation has come up." He shifted his eyes at Takeda.

Takeda took the cue. "On the evening of the Autumn Festival, Kwantung Army Lieutenant General Yoshiro Kazuki will be a special guest of Wang Jing-Wei's minister of trade and commerce, Liu Kun. Liu invited Kazuki to dinner at his home to celebrate."

Wen-Ying winced. Liu Kun. Shen Yi's husband. The traitors who now lived in the former Yuan villa.

Kazuki. The crueler-than-beast murderer under whom thousands were raped and massacred in Nanking.

They invited that Japanese demon into her old home.

"Tang Wei, secretary of propaganda for Wang's administration, will be there too," Takeda said.

Tang Wei! Wen-Ying clenched her fist. How could he? Her brother went to secondary school with him and worked with him. He saw Tang as one of his closest friends, until Tang turned and became a collaborator.

Inhuman. All of them.

"I'll be joining them that night as Kazuki's official translator,"

Takeda continued. "And unofficially, to observe and monitor Liu Kun." He tensed and lowered his voice. "This will be our chance to assassinate Kazuki."

Assassinate Kazuki? Wen-Ying raised her clenched fist.

"And to punish the traitors," Dai Li added. "We'll get rid of all of them."

Wen-Ying held her breath. She despised Liu Kun, Shen Yi, and Tang Wei. But get rid of them? Shen Yi, who she knew since birth? Tang Wei, who she once looked up to as much as she did her own older brother? Could she?

Her heart pounded.

Yes. She could.

Her breaths calmed. Slowly, her chest and shoulders eased.

Liu Kun and Shen Yi betrayed their own people. Getting rid of them would be a deliverance of justice on behalf of Heaven.

And Tang Wei? A bitter smile came to her face. She wanted him dead more than anyone else. If he hadn't joined Wang Jing-Wei's regime and become a puppet for the Japanese, Mei Mei would still be here today.

They all deserved to die.

Let them all go to hell.

"On that night, when they're full with food and drunk with alcohol, we will trap them in the dining room," Dai Li said. "And then, we'll burn down the house."

Burn down the house?

The words knocked Wen-Ying over like a blast of wind. Her old house. The last standing monument that could still remind her every day that her family once proudly held its place in this city. This country.

Her body shivered, though no one noticed. Dai Li waved his hand for the man he brought with him to come forward. "Bao Gong, say your greeting to everyone."

Bao Gong?

Bao Gong was what people called the legendary Song Dynasty

magistrate Bao Qing Tian. *Bao* was his surname. *Gong* was how one generally addressed an old man who was a respected elder. The legendary Bao Gong's fame arose from his exceptional skills in administrating justice.

The man who Dai Li called stepped up to the table. "Pleased to receive your advice," he said. His humble tone and deliberate manners contrasted sharply with his rough exterior.

"Bao Gong has been Liu Kun's head cook for fifteen years. Everyone calls him Bao Gong. He makes phenomenal steam buns." Dai Li's face cracked a rare smile. "Liu Kun takes a lot of pride in having him in his kitchen."

So that was it. A play on words. *Bao* also meant buns, so *Bao Gong* could literally mean "Elder Bun." Those who knew this man must have given him this nickname as a compliment to equate his bun-making skills to the historical *Bao Gong's* excellent skills as a judge.

Haung's stomach growled. Yu-Lan stifled a chuckle and the atmosphere in the room eased.

"Bao Gong has been working for me for four years," Dai Li continued. "Because of him, we know Liu Kun's every move."

Wen-Ying peered at the cook. This man was a mole? Everywhere, people were starving. Someone like him should be deeply loyal to Liu Kun. He should be thankful for having a job with a still prosperous household. Why was he risking his own fortune?

Dai Li. This omnipotent mastermind. Bao Gong didn't look coerced. What did Dai Li do to convince the cook to switch to their side?

"Boa Gong will make the fire look accidental like it came from the kitchen," Dai Li said. "Your group will be in charge to trap the targets and set the house on fire."

"What about the maids and houseboys? And the kitchen staff?" Wen-Ying asked. The house wasn't merely a structure. When she lived in that big mansion, her family had a house full of servants. Together, they all gave the mansion a living, beating heart. The stories of their lives formed its spirit and soul.

"To the extent he can," Dai Li said, "Bao Gong will hustle the servants and staff out of the house to spare their lives. However, we will not hold our plan for them. Hopefully, they'll come out of this alive."

Wen-Ying wrenched her fingers. So not only the house would be destroyed. There could be casualties. Her glorious old home would soon be a living cemetery where demons and innocents would be burned alive.

She shuddered at the thought.

Fan Yong-Hao always regretted missions that risked innocent lives, even though he couldn't avoid them. No one was ever as troubled about hurting the innocents as Fan. Maybe the others were too preoccupied with the failure or success of each mission to pay attention to anything else. But she could always see the guilt eating Fan up inside. Each time innocent people died at his hand, an invisible weight bore him down. Heaven had spared her from having to join them to carry out their missions and feel such torment. But they all took a vow to be brothers and sisters. Why was she allowed to escape the guilt?

Dai Li glanced at her, as though he had read her thoughts. He reminded everyone, "To take out Kazuki, sacrificing a few lives will be unavoidable."

"You said to trap them and set a fire," Huang said. "How will we get our people in there to do that?"

"Zhang Yu-Lan," Dai Li directed the question at the only other woman in the room.

Yu-Lan straightened her back. "The Lius and my family are well acquainted. Earlier in the week, when Shen Yi came to my house to play mahjong with the ladies, she was boasting about General Kazuki coming to her home for dinner on the night of the Autumn Festival. I paid her a visit yesterday. I suggested she hire the entertainment troupe who performed at my grandfather's sixtieth grand birthday banquet." She looked nervously at everyone at the table. "The troupe members aren't only performers. They're our secret agents. Performing is their way of infiltrating the collaborators' homes to gather information about the houses they live in, who they associate with, and anything else we might want to know. Sending them to the homes of Wang Jing-Wei's high officials is something I've been doing for the past year."

"You never told us this." Wen-Ying raised her brows. Yao Kang and Huang Jia-Ming, too, widened their eyes.

"Fan Da Ge thought the fewer people knew, the better." Yu-Lan ducked her head.

Dai Li spoke again. "The performance will be in three acts. First, a duet by two Peking opera singers. Then, a solo *guqin* concert, followed by a mask changer. There will be supporting musicians, as well as make-up artists. We need you to gather Tian Di Hui members to fill the roles of prop movers, runners, and assistants that night."

"You mean we'll be imposters," said Huang.

"Yes. Some Tian Di Hui members will enter Liu Kun's home as part of the troupe. Others will enter as temporary kitchen help. This will get you all past the security guards. Kerosene will be delivered to the house throughout the week before that night as part of ordinary kitchen supplies. Bao Gong will see to it the fuel is properly received. During the performances, you will subdue the guards surrounding the house, spread the kerosene, and set the house ablaze. You will set fire to all the doorways except for your own predetermined escape route so that no one in the dining room can escape."

No one in the dining room? "What about Takeda?" Wen-Ying asked.

"I'll find an excuse to leave the room before they realize the house is on fire." Takeda said before anyone else could answer.

"Not only him," Dai Li added. "The fire must be lit at exactly the right time to allow the mask changer to leave the room. His safety is a priority. He's instrumental to this ruse and we'll have use for him in the future."

And just like that, the plan was already in place. Without Fan at the helm, Dai Li had taken the liberty to direct them as he wished.

Quietly, Wen-Ying studied Yao Kang. Toward Dai Li, Yao showed only deference. Every time Dai Li spoke, he nodded in agreement without question. If Yao became their new leader, would their branch of Tian-Di Hui retain any independence?

"General Dai," Yao Kang said, "You can rest assured. I will definitely handle this matter with great care."

Dai Li gave him a cold glance. "I haven't decided who will be in charge yet. This, in fact, is the question I've gathered you all here to discuss."

An instant tension spread through the room. Yao Kang twitched his face, but kept a conciliatory grin. "General, perhaps you're not familiar with our rules. Since I'm Tian Di Hui's second in command in Shanghai, naturally I'll be leading our group now that Fan Yong-Hao has passed—"

"I'm aware Tian Di Hui has succession protocol," Dai Li cut him off. "Right now, who will take over as your leader is irrelevant to me. The only thing I care about is this plan's success. I'm still weighing whether I should entrust this mission to you or someone else."

Yao Kang's face turned deep red. "Someone else? Who else could handle such a huge, important task?"

Dai Li shot his eyes to the other side of the table. "Huang Jia-Ming?"

Startled, Huang tensed his face. The room turned dead quiet.

This was not good. Wen-Ying threw Takeda a glance. He looked back at her, his eyes reflecting the same worry.

"Do you think you're up for the job?" Dai Li asked Huang.

Huang pressed his lips. Wen-Ying could see him struggling to find a way to say yes without offending Yao Kang.

"How can he be in charge?" Yao Kang asked, ignoring Huang's hopeful yet conceding gaze. "I've seen him in action many times. He makes too many rash decisions. His temperament is still that of an immature young man. If we rely on his judgment, he'll get us all killed."

"That's not true!" Huang retorted. "It's you who will get us killed. You can't see it when things go awry and you can't think on your feet."

"How dare you talk back to me?"

"I've held my silence too long. I did it out of respect for Fan Yong-Hao. Now, I can't idly watch us go down the wrong path." He raised his head at Dai Li. "General, if you choose me, I will put Kazuki and all the treacherous rats down to death's floor. I will obliterate that house. I will burn it to ashes."

Wen-Ying glanced up. Obliterate that house? Burn it to ashes? Who was Huang Jia-Ming to make these bold claims? Did he know that house was a symbol of Chinese prestige in Shanghai? A show of equal wealth and power to the Western foreigners who had taken their land? To let them know the Chinese could still rise?

But all that is gone now...

Silence! She shouted at the voice in her head. And yet, that voice wouldn't stop. None of that mattered now, did it? It taunted her. In this war-worn city, even the Western foreigners had long since raised their white flag of defeat. What Chinese prestige was there to speak of, when the Japanese had made them kneel at their feet?

"He's not the right person, General," Yao Kang pleaded with Dai Li. Wen-Ying glared at him but he didn't notice. "Please think thrice. Tian Di Hui still stands today because we abide by our rules. If you choose Huang to lead a mission over me, our members will not accept it. If we don't follow ranks and rules, our organization will fall apart. There'll be chaos. Our brothers and sisters will rebel."

"They won't rebel," Huang fired back. Wen-Ying threw her glare over to him. "Many of our brothers and sisters have been questioning your ability to lead. Given the chance, they'll give their support to the right candidate to take the seat of the First Helm. You are not the right person."

Wen-Ying watched them argue. Neither of them was the right person. At least not the right person to burn down her house. The former Yuan villa was her ancestral home. No one had the right to touch it. Liu Kun and Shen Yi had no right to occupy it. Dai Li had no right to order it demolished. Yao Kang and Huang Jia-Ming had no right to destroy it. If anyone was entitled to take it down, it should be her.

It's time to let it go. That voice in her head whispered.

Yes. It was time. Let the house do its part to bring an end to this drawn-out, miserable battle against Japan. Let the fire consume and swallow the evil invaders and traitors in a red blazing flame.

But if the house must be obliterated, then let it be burned down by her own hands, on her terms.

"I'll do it," she said, interrupting Yao and Huang who were still arguing. Everyone stopped and turned to look at her.

"I'll do it," she said again, her voice clear and firm. "I'll bring our group in to burn Kazuki alive."

Astonished, they stared at her. Takeda's mouth fell agape.

Yao Kang recovered first. "What nonsense are you talking about? You can't lead a plan of attack."

"Yes, I can. I am the best-suited person for this job. I grew up in that house. I lived there almost my entire life. I know it better than any of you. I know it better than Liu Kun and Shen Yi. When I close my eyes, I can see every door, every hallway, every mark on the wall and every view of the windows. I know every tree and every flower planted outside, only they're now almost all dead."

She stared straight at Dai Li. "You won't find anyone who knows better than me how to quickly trap the opponents and the best way to get our people out."

Dai Lee cocked his head and studied her. A note of intrigue crept up to his eyes. "That makes sense."

"Wen-Ying." Huang shook his head. "An attack is very risky. It's too dangerous for you."

"I'll agree with him there," Yao Kang said to Dai Li. "You can't choose her. How can we let a woman lead an attack?"

Ignoring them, Wen-Ying kept her gaze on Dai Li. The corner of his lips curled up into a curious half smile as he crossed his arms and rubbed his chin. "I've always been impressed by your brother." He focused his attention on her, ignoring everyone else in the room. "Even if compared to Fan Yong-Hao, Yuan Guo-Hui wouldn't lose any luster at all. If your brother were here, I would trust him to take the lead without question."

Hearing Dai Li praise her brother, a sea of sadness stormed inside her. She thought of Guo-Hui all the time. Every day. She didn't even know if she would ever see him again.

She lifted her chin. If Guo-Hui were here, he would not let anyone else besides him burn down their house. Of that, she had no doubt.

"That house is my ancestral home," she said, still holding Dai Li's gaze. "It belongs to my family. No one here has the right to burn it down. Except me."

"Even so," Huang said, worries washing over his face, "Liu Kun's wife knows you, doesn't she? How will you enter the house? What if she sees you and recognizes you?"

Wen-Ying dug her nail into her palm. How would she hide from Shen Yi? There had to be a way.

"She can be in disguise," Yu-Lan said. "The opera singers will be in heavy make-up. We can paint her face to look the same as the *hua dan,* the lead female singer."

Wen-Ying gave her a grateful smile. Yu-Lan acknowledged it

with an encouraging squeeze of her arm.

At the head of the table, Dai Li's lips widened into a full smile. "Very good," he said to Wen-Ying. "You have drive. In my eyes, women are not inferior. There are only inferior people." He glanced at Yao Kang, then turned his sight back to Wen-Ying. "If you're half as capable as your brother, then you're more than capable of leading this attack. I'll leave this in your hands." He glared sharply at Yao Kang and Huang Jia-Ming. "Are there any objections?"

Huang twisted his lips, then relaxed his stance. "No. I'll support Yuan Wen-Ying every way I can." He leaned back and smirked at Yao Kang.

Yao Kang hugged his crossed arms close to his chest. His tight face alternately flushed with different shades of red. Grudgingly, he said, "Since it's her house, I have no objection. But let me clarify, this is not a permanent arrangement for who will succeed as the head of Tian Di Hui."

"You can take that matter up with your elders," Dai Li scowled. He turned back to Wen-Ying. "I'll leave the details up to you and Bao Gong then." He put on his hat, and left the room.

The door closed. Beneath the table, Wen-Ying locked her fingers. The burden of what she had volunteered to do had just now begun to sink in. Bao Gong, Huang Jia-Ming, Zhang Yu-Lan, all watched her with anticipation, waiting for her to give them her first word.

At the front of the table, Yao Kang looked like he could slaughter her. For a moment, she almost regretted standing in his way.

Standing beside Yao Kang, Takeda gave her a subtle nod. He smiled at her. Pride glinted in his eyes, and his face glowed with hope. Instantly, her doubts vanished. She didn't care what anyone else thought. His smile was all she needed. As long as she had Takeda behind her, she could find the strength to go on and do what needed to be done. Nothing else mattered.

CHAPTER 8

A WEEK later at the secret meeting room at Dr. Wu's clinic, Wen-Ying gathered with Bao Gong, Zhang Yu-Lan, and Takeda to show them the hand-drawn map of the inside of her old home. Yesterday, she had already met with Yao Kang, Huang Jia-Ming, and the Tian Di Hui members who would be executing the arson and assassinations. Today, she wanted to coordinate the plans for those managing people outside of their group.

This mission could not fail. When the old Yuan villa burned to ashes and the bodies of the enemy and traitors roasted in the searing fire of hell, it would be her ultimate tribute to her father, her mother, and her most beloved sister. When that happened, their souls in Heaven could rest in peace.

She had to hold it all together. The rift between her, Yao Kang, and Huang Jia-Ming could not spread any further. For the sake of Tian Di Hui, and for the sake of everything they had worked for.

Fan Yong-Hao would be so disappointed if he saw them hooking hearts and knocking horns, bickering and clashing against each other.

Maybe, a successful mission would raise everyone's spirits and unite their hearts.

Leaning over the map, Wen-Ying pushed her palms against the top of the table. "The villa's dining room is situated north." She circled her finger around the big room in the middle of the first floor. "There are three entrances. One to the main drawing room in the front. One to the corridor leading to the kitchen, and one to the hallway to the back stairwell. The back stairway is used by servants. It also leads to the staff's entrance at the back of the house."

She checked everyone's reaction around the table to make sure they understood. In wealthy households, staff members and vendors were required to use a separate door to enter and exit the building. Main doors were reserved for use only by members of the family and their guests.

"On the night of the Mid-Autumn Festival, Bao Gong will bring Yao Kang, Huang Jia-Ming, and four of our Tian Di Hui members into the kitchen as temporary help. I, Zhang Yu-Lan, and four other members will enter the house in disguise as part of the performance troupe."

She pointed to the sitting room near the back stairway. "Boa Gong, this room is the most convenient for the performance troupe to wait and prepare. It's also the closest to the staff entrance. You should advise Shen Yi to allow the troupe to use this room that night."

"That should be no problem," Bao Gong said. Wen-Ying didn't think it would be either. That sitting room, being so close to the kitchen and the staff's common room, was the least used even when her own family occupied the house.

"The staff entrance will be our escape route," she said. "It'll be the last door to be sealed off." She picked up a second folded copy of the map and gave it to Yu-Lan. "Be sure the performers know where the escape door is and how they will go outside. They should leave as soon as their performance is over."

"I will." Yu-Lan accepted the map, but Wen-Ying held on. Yu-Lan frowned with a quizzical look.

"Are you sure you want to come along?" Wen-Ying asked. Yu-Lan had volunteered to join them that night to help direct the escape of the theater troupe and to provide moral support. She and Wen-Ying planned to disguise themselves as understudies for the Peking opera singers. That would enable them to enter the mansion with their faces fully painted to avoid being recognized. "You don't have to come in person."

"I know." Yu-Lan pulled the copy of the map. "I want to come."

"Why?" Wen-Ying couldn't understand. In the past, all their larger and more dangerous resistance missions had been against Japanese officials and at places where the Imperial Japanese Army operated. When they attacked collaborators, they had always targeted their offices, their vehicles, or in public places. Poison in a restaurant, stabbing in a lounge, murder in a hotel room, even shoot-outs on the streets. This was the first time they attempted arson in a family home. Yu-Lan had to have considered the implications. "What if next time, we target your family? In your home?"

Yu-Lan grimaced. "I've thought of this point as well. My parents aren't political, even though they've made the choice to support Wang Jing-Wei. They're just greedy and selfish. They always have been. They only look out for themselves. And my brothers? They're just like my parents. All of them are cowards who are willing to accept humiliation to stay alive. But for all their faults, they are not evil. Not like Liu Kun. They don't torture or murder our own kind." She lifted her head. Her eyes a mixture of determination and fear. "Evil can't win against the good. I believe the Japanese and the traitors are destined to lose. I'm doing what I do because if the day comes when Tian Di Hui decides to eliminate my family, I can ask for clemency for them. Maybe after all that I've done for Tian Di Hui, the ones who will make the final decision will grant them mercy on my account."

Wen-Ying softened her face. She never knew. Deep inside, Yu-

Lan still cared greatly about her family, and she had found a way to keep her familial devotion while honoring her vows and upholding her loyalty to Tian Di Hui.

Takeda and Bao Gong stared at Wen-Ying, waiting for her to speak.

"What if the Tian Di Hui elders refuse?" Wen-Ying asked. "What if they don't grant your family clemency?"

"Then, they only have themselves to blame. But I would know I had made my best efforts to save them, and I can't not try."

Wen-Ying let go of the copy of the map. She would not be able to change Yu-Lan's mind. Neither did she want to. In her place, Wen-Ying herself would have done the same thing.

"All right." She brought everyone's attention back to their plan. "After dinner is served, the performers will begin the entertainment in the dining room."

As she said this, her memory flashed back to entertainers who had come through her house over the years. Puppeteers her parents had paid to perform on her eleventh birthday. Singers, dancers, jugglers. Back then, their home was always bustling with activities.

They didn't only hire Chinese performers either. Sometimes, they would invite pianists and violinists. For her forty-fourth birthday, her mother had refused a banquet celebration, which her father proposed. The number four was considered a bad omen because it was pronounced the same as the word "death" in Chinese. Her mother, who was always overly superstitious, didn't want to tempt fate with a banquet. So instead of a big celebration, Mei Mei invited a classmate to perform a piano and violin concerto together with her as a birthday gift after a sumptuous feast for the family at home.

The sound of Mei Mei's piano music would grace this world no more…

"Wen-Ying?" Takeda called her name.

Wen-Ying came out of her thoughts. "Bao Gong will bring Yao Kang, Huang Jia-Ming, and four other Tian Di Hui members as one team into the house earlier in the day as temporary kitchen staff. When the performers begin their first act, Yao Kang and Huang will lead their team to get rid of the security guards outside."

She drew a deep breath. From this point on, all their lives would be at risk. But if she could rely on Yao Kang and Huang for anything, it was their well-honed skill to silently kill. "After that, I will lead my team to pour kerosene in front of all the doors and windows on the first floor. We'll begin with the doors and windows leading to the outside, and work our way to the interior doors. We'll trap everyone inside the dining room. Once the fire starts, Kazuki and his henchmen, Liu Kung and his wife, and Tang Wei will have no route to escape." She paused. The finality of her own words chilled her own spine.

"Bao Gong?"

"Yes?"

"The mask changer will be the final act." She moved the red and black painted mask of an angry face on the table to the center. "When he switches his mask to this one, it is our signal. You will start the smoke in the kitchen and call for the house staff to escape. Yao Kang and Huang Jia-Ming will stay behind and pretend to put out the fire. Try to save as many innocents as you can." She bit her lip, then pushed on. "Takeda, that's also your signal to get out. It should take a while before the smoke drifts into the dining room."

"Understood," Takeda answered. A thousand words were spoken between them in the moment he met her gaze.

Danger. The warning shot into her mind, breaking the magic. Wen-Ying looked away and forced her fear to the side. Of course there would be danger. The mission was a risk to all of them. Takeda would be fine. He had one of the easiest roles in this whole set up. She shouldn't worry about him more than she worried about everyone else. If she were to be a leader, she could not let her personal feelings interfere.

She understood now why Fan Yong-Hao remained unmarried. He could not favor any person above another. He could not have private emotions that might sway his actions or thoughts.

"When the performer puts on this mask, we'll have ten minutes to light all the fires except for the doorways to the dining room and the servants' entrance. The servants' entrance will be our escape route." She pointed at the spot on the map. "Once the mask changer leaves the dining room, he'll head straight for escape, and we'll set fire to seal all three dining room exits."

The room fell silent. Wen-Ying put down her hand next to the mask. What words of comfort or encouragement should she say? She was so ill-prepared to be the one to inspire the others.

Takeda spoke up, reciting one of Tian Di Hui's sacred vows. "Three knives, six eyes, no room for mercy. A pledge to eliminate the enemy, one swipe to empty all."

Wen-Ying looked up. Those words. Takeda understood. She understood. Until they succeeded, until they drove out their enemy—every last one of them, these words were what they would live for. These words would be their anchor. Their light to guide them out of the reign of darkness.

CHAPTER 9

HOLDING on to the lamp post, Wen-Ying gazed at her old home. This time, to memorize every detail she could. After tomorrow, the once grand Yuan family villa would be no more.

"It's difficult to let go, isn't it?" Takeda said behind her.

"The people aren't there anymore," she said. Not the people who mattered anyway. "What use is it to leave behind a house." Her denial hardly convinced herself. He must have known she was lying too, for he put a comforting hand on her shoulder.

"There's nothing left of it now. It's just an empty shell. Everything inside is gone." She gritted her teeth. She had to say this, so she could steel her own heart and do what she must when the time came.

Takeda looked on with sad, sympathetic eyes. "When the Japanese soldiers took over the city, they looted everything from all the abandoned houses."

That wasn't what she meant. "There's no soul inside the house anymore. No traditions to uphold. No music to enliven the world. No legacy worth carrying on." Nothing. The family that gave this house its soul no longer dwelled within. Her father was no longer there to pass on his wisdom. Her mother no longer there to burn incense for the ancestral shrine. Mei Mei's laughter no longer warmed the corridors. Even if her brother, Guo Hui, could return one day and reclaim it, he could never pass it on to his children as the symbol of pride for all that the name Yuan represented. Evil spirits now occupied this place. Twisted, depraved spirits. All the holy water in the world could not wash such evil away.

Sourness swelled in the back of her throat. She swallowed and blinked back the stinging tears.

"That balcony." Takeda pointed to the west side of the villa's third floor. "Was that where you and your sister used to go to watch the moon?"

Wen-Ying followed the direction of his finger. "Yes. On the nights of the Autumn Festival. How'd you guess?"

Takeda smiled. "It's the only balcony with a cypress tree next to it."

The cypress tree. This giant wonder that had seen so much over the years. It still stood, glorious and robust, untouched by the dark evil that had swept these grounds. It was the only living thing remaining in this villa that could still wave its claim of innocence despite the wickedness infesting this place.

"By tomorrow night, that tree too will burn to ashes," she said. It broke her heart to know she would be the one to take its life away.

"Maybe not all of it." Takeda pulled her back against him.

"What do you mean?"

"See those branches hanging over the balcony?"

"Yes?"

"Tomorrow night, I'll try to take one of the branches. If I can sneak up there without anyone's notice, I'll bring you back a branch."

"No." Wen-Ying turned her head around. "That's not part of the plan. Don't risk it."

"It'll be fine," he said. "I'll have ten minutes from when I leave the dining room till you set the house fully on fire. That's plenty of time. It'll be easy."

"Takeda!" She raised her hand to his chest to stop him.

"Let me handle this." He grabbed her fist and closed it in his own. "I know you want this. It'll be a token. Something you can keep to remember your sister by."

Slowly, Wen-Ying relented. She turned her gaze back at the tree and the balcony. A gust of wind blew above the house and the cypress tree's leaves fluttered like a thousand butterflies' wings. According to legend, a tree that lived to a thousand years old would grow a spirit. The spirit would take on human form and acquire magical powers. Other myths and folklore also said that sometimes, when a person died, his spirit would survive and merge with something living around them. Like a bird, or a flower, or a tree.

She didn't know how many years the cypress tree had lived. But could she grasp on to the belief that Mei Mei's spirit was still alive? Could she hold on to the hope that Mei Mei's body had left for the Heavens, but her soul had merged with the tree, and she was now the tree's spirit? If so, her spirit would protect them when they carried out their plan, wouldn't it?

"We're going to succeed," Takeda whispered in her ear. "Tomorrow, we'll wipe them all out."

CHAPTER 10

A NIGHT OF FULL MOON.

Here on earth, the Autumn Festival elicited no excitement or joy. Starvation plagued the country, and no one wanted to think about mooncakes. The bells of curfew rang, and families hustled their children inside. None could frolic with their festival lanterns on the streets after dark.

And yet, above in the sky, the silhouette of Chang 'e looked clearer than ever in the luminous celestial light. This elusive goddess who, in a haste to break free from her assailant, deserted the mortal bond of love. As she sailed across the sky, chasing the moon, did she think to look down even once to see how much the people below were suffering? Wen-Ying wondered as their caravan approached the road leading to the former Yuan mansion.

She pulled her gaze back from the heavens to her own reflection on the glass of the vehicle's window. No time to admire the moon now. Tonight, she had come to end once and for all the celebration of this holiday at the house she could no longer call home. She had taken on the disguise as one of the singers coming to perform a scene from the famous romantic Peking opera *Peony*

Pavilion. Along with Zhang Yu-Lan, they would enter the target location as understudies. Wen-Ying herself for the female lead, and Zhang Yu-Lan for the male lead.

Wen-Ying touched her cheek with her fingertip. The make-up artist did a fantastic job. The thick white paint on her face, the crimson red paint on her lips and around her eyes, and the heavy wig hid her appearance so well, she could not recognize herself.

Next to her, Yu-Lan folded her hands on her lap. "Don't worry. I'm certain we'll succeed."

Wen-Ying hoped so. "How were you able to come out tonight anyway? Doesn't your family expect you to celebrate the Mid-Autumn Festival with them?"

"Ha!" Yu-Lan laughed, then lowered her voice not to disturb the others sitting in the back. "After Dai Li told me about tonight's mission, I convinced my parents to take the whole family to celebrate at our villa out in the countryside. My father recently bought the summer villa that used to belong to the British Taipan Tony Keswick. I told him the moon would shine brighter out there away from the city. When they were all ready to head out yesterday, I pretended I fell ill."

"And they left without you? They aren't worried you're home, sick and all alone?"

"My mother didn't want to go without me. But they had no choice. I made sure of that. After they decided to celebrate out in the villa, I talked my parents into inviting her three mahjong pals and their husbands. It didn't take much convincing on my part. My mother was eager to show off our new countryside retreat. Since her friends would all be arriving, they had to leave without me. I told them I would try to join them today if I felt better." She flicked her eyes from left to right. "I guess I'm still ill." She stuck out her tongue.

"You little mischievous spirit. You've been planning this," Wen-Ying said. "You meant to come with us all along!"

Yu-Lan smiled in admission. "When my maidservant brought me my soup for dinner tonight, I told her I needed rest. I told her she was strictly not to let anyone bother me in my room unless I called for them. Then I sneaked out through my bedroom window."

"Are you sure no one will discover you're gone?"

"Of course I'm sure!" she said. Then, her face dropped. "Our servants hate us. They submit to us because they need work. They need the pay and working for people like us will guarantee that. But they know we're traitors, and they hate us for having so much and living so well when they and everybody else are struggling to survive. If they could feed us to dogs, they would."

"Yu-Lan." Wen-Ying touched her on the back. "That's not true."

"Yes, it is. Anyway, none of them would want to exert an extra ounce of effort for us. With my whole family gone and I specifically told them not to bother me, they'd all be glad to have a night off."

Wen-Ying knew Yu-Lan was speaking the truth. How ironic. In occupied China, it seemed the life of a young lady of a prosperous family wasn't so wonderful either.

This evil war. It turned everyone against each other. Everybody was bearing humiliation for the sake of survival.

"I don't want to stay on the side watching all the time," Yu-Lan said. "I took the vow to defend us all as real blood brothers and sisters. Now that Fan Da Ge's no longer here, I want to put in more effort, to do my share, if that can help. Besides, with both Yao Kang and Huang Jia-Ming fighting in the open and scheming in the dark for the seat of the First Helm, you need someone who will think only of supporting you. That's what I'm here for."

The driver turned his head slightly and said to Wen-Ying. "We've arrived."

Wen-Ying nodded. As they pulled into the driveway, her

stomach twisted. It'd been more than a year since she last set foot onto these grounds. Tonight, she would claim this place back. The unwitting occupants inside didn't know it, but tonight, everyone here were puppets, and she held all the strings. Starting now, she would be the master of this place again.

The vehicle stopped and the driver got out to open the door. Behind him, stone-faced Japanese guards peered into the vehicle. Wen-Ying exchanged a glance with the leader of the troupe, the mask changer. Quietly, he climbed out, followed by the *guqin* performer. The two Peking Opera singers looked at Wen-Ying. Then they, too, left. Wen-Ying nudged Yu-Lan. Bowing their heads, they exited with the musicians and drummer who would provide musical accompaniment for the opera performance and the mask changing act.

Behind them on the driveway, their second vehicle arrived, carrying the troupe's staff, costumes, musical instruments, and equipment. One by one, the make-up artist, the costumes manager, and Tian Di Hui members posing as troupe hands got out.

A middle-aged man in Chinese *tangzhuan* uniform came running out of the house. "I'm coming, I'm coming," he shouted. With his authoritative manners, Wen-Ying guessed he must be Liu Kun's head houseboy.

How did the bamboo grow another branch? They couldn't afford an added diversion. Neither Dai Li nor Bao Gong mentioned the head houseboy. Bao Gong was supposed to make arrangements to get the household staff out of their way. This houseboy could be a problem if he stayed around. What would she do if he took it upon himself to direct their coming and going?

She could think of no solution for now but to take it one step at a time.

Not shaken in the least, the troupe leader walked up to the

houseboy and greeted him. The houseboy flung his sleeve. "You're all here to perform tonight?" he demanded to know.

"Yes," said the troupe leader. That seasoned old hand. He didn't show any bit of worry or nerves.

The guards pointed at the trunks the troupe hands wanted to unload.

The houseboy went toward the trunks. "What are those?"

"Costumes, musical instruments, some equipment—"

"Open them."

The troupe leader gestured at their team to do as they were told. While the commotion was happening, Wen-Ying kept her head low. She wasn't worried about their trunks. The materials they really needed—the kerosene and guns—Bao Gong already brought them in by hiding them with the kitchen deliveries earlier in the week before the Japanese guards arrived. The only things hidden in their trunks were the Japanese army uniforms stored in concealed compartments. Those would come into play later.

What did upset her was seeing the guards yanking open the trunks and roughly shifting and tossing all the items inside. Such outright disrespect. They did this on purpose too, she was sure. What angered her even more was watching the houseboy standing there, grinning at the Japanese dogs while sneering at his own kind. It took all her self-restraint to keep quiet.

The troupe leader, however, stepped forward. "Of course, it's a small matter to us if our costumes and equipment are accidentally damaged," he said to the houseboy. "But if something happens and we can't put on our best performance tonight, General Kazuki might be very unhappy."

The houseboy's face immediately changed. Quickly, he went up to the guards. Waving his hands for them to stop, he repeated again and again, "For Kazuki. For Kazuki."

Wen-Ying sucked in her cheeks. It would not do for her to show she enjoyed watching them squirm.

Looking uncertain, the guards exchanged a few words, then backed off and pointed them to the path of the staff entrance.

The troupe leader led everyone to gather and move forward. All the while, his face betrayed not a hint of anything out of the ordinary. Wen-Ying couldn't help admire how he handled the whole ordeal. She must learn to stay calm under pressure like him.

The pompous houseboy continued his menace. "This way," he shouted at them. "This house has rules. People cannot wander around alone, especially not a group of actors like you. I'll warn you all now. If I find any valuable item missing after tonight, your whole group will have to answer to Master Liu and Madam Liu."

Wen-Ying glowered at his back. What did this running dog know about things that were valuable? Once, before the war, her family had owned some of the finest treasure money could buy. Why would she want any of the Lius' inferior properties? What a joke.

This prick of a houseboy. How could they get rid of him?

The houseboy led them to the sitting room where Wen-Ying suggested. All right. At least Bao Gong took care of that part.

"You're to stay in here until you're called to perform," the houseboy wagged his finger. "I will not—"

"Good evening!" Bao Gong entered and interrupted him. "Welcome. I'm the head cook here. The master and madam of the house have kindly instructed me to bring you all mooncakes to share." He stepped aside to make way for the woman behind him carrying a tray of mooncakes cut to wedges on plates. A girl, about sixteen, brought in a pot of tea and cups.

Ignoring the mooncakes, Wen-Ying eyed Bao Gong and tossed her head slightly at the houseboy, but Bao Gong wouldn't look directly at her. He came toward them with a smile.

Was Bao Gong betraying them? Wen-Ying's palms started to sweat.

The women and the girl laid the mooncakes and tea on the

table. The troupe stared longingly at the snacks. Like most people, they hadn't eaten anything sweet for a very long time.

"Ahem." The houseboy cleared his throat. "I haven't finished talking. Don't any of you disappoint our master and madam after how well they're treating you tonight. I will not tolerate—" He stopped. His eyes bulged. Then, to everyone's surprise, he yowled and bowed over.

"Uncle Rong! What's the matter?" The woman rushed over to his side, but the houseboy continued to moan. He held both his hands over his stomach as the woman helped him to the sofa. "Wah!" she exclaimed. "You're spilling cold sweat."

"My stomach..." he uttered, squeezing his eyes.

"Did you eat something bad?" Bao Gong asked. "I know. You must've gone to Old Zhu's shop again. I told you not to go there. Their dog meat hot pots aren't clean."

The houseboy scrunched his face and bared his teeth in pain.

"We can't let this interrupt the feast," said the woman. "Madam will be furious if she found out you got yourself sick tonight. You better go back to your room. Little Yin!" she said to the teenage girl. "Go get Ah Three."

"Yes." The girl left on her order.

"Uncle Rong," the woman said to the houseboy, patting his back. "You go get some rest. I'll cover for you. I'll supervise this group of actors and our staff. We must not let Madam know about this."

The girl returned with a younger houseboy of lower rank.

"Ah Three," the woman said to the younger houseboy. "Uncle Rong is ill. Take him back to his room to get some rest."

Startled, the servant Ah Three rushed to help. "Yes."

The head houseboy, whose face had turned pale white, was now in too much agony to object.

After they left, the girl Little Yin covered her mouth and giggled. Wen-Ying scowled at Bao Gong. What was going on?

Bao Gong came closer to her. "Allow me to introduce. This is my wife, Ah Xia." He pointed at the woman, who gave everyone a warm smile. "And that's my daughter, Little Yin." The girl wiggled her brows and grinned.

Wen-Ying relaxed with a sigh. The houseboy was gone. Could they be this lucky? She looked at Bao Gong askance. "Do you have a hand in this?"

"Me?" He pointed at himself, indignant. "What do I have to do with him eating dog meat?" He asked, but his conspiratorial smile told her otherwise. His face then turned serious. "Ah Xia will make sure most of our staff remain in their common room after the feast is over and before the performances start. With such an important guest here, they can't be wandering around anyhow, and they need to be in one place where they can quickly respond if they're called on. This should get them out of your way, as well as making it easier to run them out of the house once the fire starts. Also, Little Yin will be the designated attendant in the dining room throughout the night." He lowered his voice and said to the troupe leader. "She will give the signal when you put on the red mask."

"Thank you." Wen-Ying looked gratefully at Ah Xia and Little Yin. Bao Gong's entire family was risking their lives. If their plan succeeded tonight, all three of them would be out of their livelihood. And yet, here they were, doing everything to help. The conviction on their faces did not waver.

There was still hope for the Chinese people yet.

Huang Jia-Ming came in, dressed in a cook's uniform. "Golden Phoenix," he called out to Wen-Ying. In operations involving outsiders, Tian Di Hui members never referred to each other by name, but rather, by their ranks or code names. "I'm sorry. White Paper Fan decided not to come tonight."

"What?" Yao Kang wasn't coming?

"He said this is a mission for lower level members. At the last minute, he told us his role as the current highest ranking member is to stay behind and supervise. He said if we fail, he will lead everyone else and decide what to do next."

"How could he?" Yu-Lan asked.

Wen-Ying wanted to ask the same. Clearly, Yao Kang meant to defy her. He wanted to show he didn't need to submit to her authority. Rather than helping them to succeed, he had decided to use this mission to stake his claim as Tian Di Hui's next leader.

All that was beside the point. What distressed her most now was that he had put their mission in jeopardy. He and Huang were supposed to lead four other members to assassinate the Japanese guards outside. They had planned on splitting into groups of two with one person shooting a guard dead and taking the body away. The other person would stand in and take the guard's place to avoid suspicions and to assist when they set the outside entrances on fire. The Japanese army uniforms hidden in the trunks' concealed compartments were brought for this specific purpose.

"I need someone on your team to take Yao Kang's place," Huang said to Wen-Ying. They looked at the three Tian Di Hui members who had come in disguised as troupe hands. She needed them too to set the house on fire.

"Take Ah Green," said Yu-Lan. Ah Green was the best shooter among the three designated to carry out the arson part of their operation with Wen-Ying. "I'll take Ah Green's place here."

Wen-Ying and Huang looked at each other, then back at Yu-Lan. It didn't feel right to task a dainty girl like her in such a role.

"There's no other solution." Yu-Lan urged. "It's the only way."

She was right. They had to make do whichever way they could now. Wen-Ying turned to her team. "Ah Green, go with Huang."

With a firm nod, Ah Green stepped forward.

"Bring out the fake uniforms," Wen-Ying ordered. The troupe

hands pulled the bags of uniforms from the trunk and gave them to Huang and Ah Green.

"Go!" she told both of them. With no further delay, Huang and Ah Green left. Everyone else in the room stared at Wen-Ying, waiting. Wen-Ying didn't know for sure what she should say, but in the air, she sensed their anxiety. They were all waiting for someone to take charge. She closed the door and walked to the center of the room. "The rest is up to us. Bao Gong, Ah Xia, Little Yin, you can return to work. We'll be fine here." She looked over everyone out the window. The warm rays of moonlight shimmered through the panes like a sign from Heaven. A surge of strength rose within her. Drawing on it, she began to find her voice. Invoking one of Tian Di Hui's covenants, she said, "Those with compassion and righteousness shall pass below the bridge. Those without compassion and righteousness shall die by our blade. We are the guardians of heaven and earth. We are *zhonghua's* sons and daughters. Tonight, no obstacle can stop us. On this full moon evening of August fifteenth, we will eliminate these beasts. You all know your roles. When the time comes, we will act according to plan."

A chorus of "yes" answered her. She could feel it. The group's determination, temporarily shaken, once again took on momentum. Their will swelled, like scattered wind coalescing around the eye of a typhoon. Together they stood, an unstoppable force driving in one direction, ready to storm those in their path.

Bao Gong gave Wen-Ying one last look. His face glowed with pride. "Take care of yourself."

"You too," Wen-Ying said. If they both survived this night, she would personally offer him an eternal promise to always come to his aide whenever he needed.

Excusing themselves, Bao Gong, his wife, and daughter left the room. Now, there was nothing left for them to do but wait.

"Watch over everyone," Wen-Ying said to Yu-Lan. "I'm going to take a look around."

"By yourself?" Yu-Lan pulled Wen-Ying's sleeve, worried.

"That's the best way. I know my way around this house. I want to scout out the place before we start."

"What if someone sees you?"

"I'll say I got lost."

Yu-Lan hesitated, then let go. "Be careful."

"I will," Wen-Ying promised, then quietly went out to the corridor.

CHAPTER 11

AFTER CHECKING LEFT and right to make sure no one was around, Wen-Ying tiptoed past the back stairway toward the dining room. The silence in the hallway and rooms felt odd for an evening when a family was planning to receive an important dignitary for a celebratory feast. Only the voices of the kitchen staff and the clings and clangs of pots and pans could be heard at the back of the house. Then again, the tight control of everyone's whereabouts made sense. In their world today, there were eyes and ears behind every wall. Liu Kun and Kazuki wouldn't want any idle people roaming around.

Quietly, Wen-Ying passed by the study. Unable to resist, she pushed open the door. To her surprise, the furniture and their arrangement remained the same, although the valuable paintings, decorative ornaments, and books on the shelves had all been replaced.

A gnashing pain wrenched her heart. This room was where her father would retreat to every night after dinner to review the accounting books. She could still hear the loud ticks and tacks of the abacus as his fingers pushed the beads at flying speed.

Closing her eyes, she shut the door and moved on.

The staff's voices grew louder as she approached the dining room. From its nearest doorway, she peeked inside to watch the servants hustling back and forth setting the table and preparing the room for tonight's feast. Again, the similarities between the dining room's decor and the way her family had arranged it surprised her. Every piece of furniture and artwork, it seemed, had remained in its place. Or rather, the old furniture and artwork were gone, likely looted by the Japanese. Instead, replicas and other similar items had been put in their place. Like the large painting of mountains and a waterfall on the main wall, and the antique porcelain vases on the console, and the golden laughing Buddha with many children on the display shelf. At first glance, she could almost believe she had stepped back in time to the Yuan's dining room.

This had to be Shen Yi's doing. Liu Kun wasn't a friend of her family. He had never been to her home. He could not have known what the interior of the Yuan mansion looked like.

Wen-Ying slid her fingers down the door frame. Goosebumps crawled on her skin. Shen Yi. This venomous woman. Her ire ran so deep. This was her act of revenge. Her parade of victory. It wasn't enough that she took over this villa and now ruled it as its mistress. She had to replicate the inside this way as if she were the rightful Madam Yuan. She would live the life owed to her, even if Guo Hui denied it from her.

Putting her thoughts of Shen Yi aside, Wen-Ying took note of the dining room's layout. Her family's beautiful hand-carved rosewood table was gone. Where it used to be, a marble dining table, framed by mahogany wood, filled the half of the room. Behind the table was the door with access to the kitchen. The other half of the room, where the performances would take place, had a door on the right and a door to the left. The door to the right led to the sitting room where the troupe was waiting and the servants' entrance. The door to the left led to the main drawing room.

If Bao Gong could keep both of those doors closed except when the performers were entering and exiting the door on the right, she and her team could pour kerosene quietly around the dining room while the targets watched the entertainment inside. When the last performers left, they would immediately seal the three doors with fire. By the time those demons realized they were trapped, the fire would quash any hope they had to escape.

Thinking about this, Wen-Ying's hands and body sweat. Hold it together, she told herself. She must hold herself together. The lives of all her Tian Di Hui brothers and sisters depended on her. And the lives of Bao Gong's family and the performance troupe too.

Those without compassion and righteousness shall die by our blade. She repeated this in her mind, trying to calm her breath.

"The General is here!" A male servant standing watch by the front door shouted. "Go tell Master and Madam."

The servants' footsteps pounded the hallway and up the front staircase toward the master bedroom. Wen-Ying looked ahead to the front door and the main drawing room, then backward at the sitting room where the troupe was confined.

Which way to go?

Abandoning the way back, she dashed up the back stairway just as Liu Kun, Shen Yi, and a maidservant were walking down the front staircase to the first floor to greet their guests. Her heart pounding, she moved as lightly as she could to the landing area at the top of the front stairs and crouched down. A servant opened the front door and the Japanese General Kazuki entered, followed by Takeda and the unforgivable traitor, Tang Wei.

Fury burned inside her as Wen-Ying looked at Tang Wei's face. The son of a bitch. He sure looked well. Healthy and in good spirit. Must be so good to have another person serve as his substitute to die in his place. Mei Mei rotting in what should have been his grave so he could live to spread lies and propaganda for the Japanese crushing his own people. This score had to be settled tonight.

Liu Kun and Shen Yi bowed to greet Kazuki, the Japanese commander. Watching them, Wen-Ying sneered. These two. Kowtowing to their oppressor and accepting humiliation on behalf of the entire country of Chinese people.

Not too big a price to pay for these two, perhaps. What was humiliation of your own kind when one could bathe in cash in exchange? Look at Shen Yi. The huge pearls of her necklace hanging like rings of iron chained around her neck. The heavy golden bracelets handcuffed around her wrists. Not to mention the diamonds on her rings. Every time she turned her hands, the sparks of the stones flashed under the ceiling light. Maybe when one exposed her eyes to such lights long enough, the eyes would turn blind. Blind to their enemy's savage cruelty, and blind to the thousands of victims' bitterness, cries, and pains.

Shen Yi gained some weight too. The body fitting silk qipao revealed not the slender shape which she once proudly showed off. Too many days spent playing incessant hours of mahjong and eating the eight treasured cuisines had rounded her out from top to bottom. Who cared if the rest of the world was starving?

Enjoy your last meal, Wen-Ying cursed Shen Yi in her thoughts. *It will be your final taste of comfort before the king of the underworld banishes you to the eighteen levels of hell.*

And Liu Kun. That one with the face of a human and the heart of a violent beast. She knew how he tortured and killed those who tried to rise up against their enemy but unfortunately got caught. The time had come for Liu Kun to pay the price for his crime.

At the front door, Takeda, acting as translator, spoke to both the hosts and the Japanese guest. A male servant came and brought slippers for the guests. Kazuki turned. For the first time, Wen-Ying got a good look at his face. She braced herself for the sight of a cold-blooded animal. Maybe a demon with eyes of a snake. But what she saw instead was a round-cheeked little man. A long, thick mustache hung above his mouth, making him look slightly comical. The creases on his forehead showed an aging uncle rather than a predator in his prime. His soft, almond-shaped eyes looked almost benign.

Not possible. Not possible. Kazuki, one of the masterminds who led thousands of troops in the rape and massacre of Nanking. How could he appear so mild? How could he have a face that elicited sympathy?

Deception. It was all a deception. Those Japanese dogs. Their faces lied. And Kazuki. That benevolent face masked the dark, evil heart of a man who brutally took hundreds of thousands of lives.

Wen-Ying grabbed a spindle. Her heart would not soften. Tonight was for all those whose lives were taken and destroyed by his hand. Tonight, she would avenge them all.

The servant put the guests' shoes neatly aside. Continuing their small talk, the guests and hosts downstairs proceeded into the main drawing room. For a brief second, Takeda glanced up. His eyes met Wen-Ying's and a shade of shock registered on his face. Instinctively, Wen-Ying held her finger to her lips. Her heart thumped. Luckily, he maintained his composure and no one noticed the slight wavering in his voice.

Did he really recognize her in her disguise?

It didn't matter. Even if he didn't, he knew she was one of the assassins tonight.

In the drawing room, Liu Kun and Shen Yi invited their guests to sit down while a maidservant brought out a tray of tea. Kazuki spoke, and Takeda said to the hosts, "The General thanks you for your great hospitality tonight."

"It is our utmost honor he would join us this evening for our Mid-Autumn Festival celebration." Liu Kun opened his palm. To better hear what they were saying, Wen-Ying kneeled lower on the floor.

Takeda repeated Liu's words to Kazuki. Serving as their intermediary, he facilitated their conversation. "The General is pleased to partake in this opportunity of cultural exchange. Going forward, he hopes China will also observe Japanese cultural practices as a way to strengthen our mutual ties and commonalities. Take for example Korea. After it became a Japanese protectorate, that region has fully embraced its new Japanese identity. Their people have adopted Japanese names. They've discontinued using the Korean language in favor of the Japanese language. Even their old royal palace had been demolished. This spirit of unity will surely help to foster the Greater Pan-Asian Co-prosperity Sphere as our great Emperor Hirohito envisioned."

Those sickening words, couched in such flowery speech. Worse yet, she had to hear them from Takeda's mouth. It hardly helped that he was merely translating someone else's words. Everyone knew Japan was actively purging Korea of its culture. They forced the Koreans to take on Japanese names and forbade them from speaking their own language. Those who refused to comply were punished. They confiscated Korean archaeological treasures and artifacts to deprive the Koreans of their entire history.

Without knowing it, Wen-Ying clenched her fist. The Japanese were delusional if they thought they could do the same to China. China would not succumb so easily yet.

Takeda put down his cup and the maid refilled his tea. Wen-Ying watched him thank the maid.

How hard it must be for him to serve as the voice of these demons day in and day out? How much strength did it take for him to hold on to faith in humanity while surrounded by these beasts? What did he need to do to keep his hope for a victorious end on their side when he had to witness every day evil hands getting their ways? She never knew the magnitude of anguish he had to go through. She didn't cherish him enough.

"The wisdom of Emperor Hirohito will benefit us all," Tang Wei said.

Wen-Ying swung her head toward him. *What did he say?*

"President Wang Jing-Wei and the Reorganized National Government of China is committed to support Emperor Hirohito in the establishment of the Pan-Asian Co-Prosperity Sphere. United, all Asiatic countries will stand as a single formidable force, never again to be disrespected by the West."

Takeda repeated in Japanese to Kazuki what Tang Wei said. Liu Kun and Shen Yi smiled and nodded in agreement as they took their tea. How Takeda could hold back his true feelings, Wen-Ying did not know. If she had a knife in her hand, she would stab Tang Wei in the heart right now with her own hands.

Kazuki then spoke at length. Sadness overtook his face. Takeda explained, "General Kazuki said, it's too bad not all Chinese think the same as you. To this day, the General deeply regrets the incidental suffering of the Chinese people when the Imperial Japanese Army had to defend themselves and the Emperor's acts of greater good for the Asiatic region. He especially regrets what happened in Nanking seven years ago. If only the Chinese understood back then like you do now what Japan was trying to achieve for all of us. If they hadn't incited the Japanese troops and put up such a fierce fight when our troops came to implement the Emperor's order, things wouldn't have gotten out of hand. The General's heart still aches when he thinks of all those who were harmed."

His heart still aches? The phony compassion of a cat crying over a mouse. Squinting at the scene down below, Wen-Ying wanted to spit in Kazuki's face before torching him in flame.

Liu Kun lowered his cup of tea. "There's no need to talk about things that happened in the past anymore. When we defeat Chiang Kai-Shek and what remains of his Nationalist Government, and when we wipe out that nail in the eye, Mao Zedong and his little red party, our new government will see to it that China will cooperate and ally with Japan in the most peaceful, orderly manner."

That human waste. How could he say such words? He wanted to put the bloodbath of Nanking behind and forget it like it didn't even warrant an afterthought?

The fire she had planned hadn't even begun, but her rage was burning inside her.

Good thing Little Yin entered to inform Shen Yi that the feast was about to begin. Wen-Ying couldn't bear to listen to any of this anymore.

Shen Yi tapped Liu Kun on the arm. He got up and invited his guests into the dining room.

Takeda waited for everyone else to walk ahead of him, then glanced up at Wen-Ying. She held up her hand and waved her fingers. His expression remained unchanged, but the tenderness in his eyes sparked a different kind of fire inside her. Silently, she vowed to herself. She would have a future with this man. She would fight their oppressors to the end for a future where he and she could live the life of freedom they deserved.

She closed her hand and held it to her heart, then opened it toward him. Takeda smiled. A barely noticeable smile only she could see. He turned his gaze away and left with the others into the dining room. When they were all gone, Wen-Ying sneaked back to the stairway from where she had come and scurried back to rejoin the troupe.

CHAPTER 12

THE FEAST LASTED ALMOST two hours. While Wen-Ying and her group waited, no one tried to make conversations. The weight of what they were about to do was enough. She had already taken a chance by wandering the house alone and eavesdropping on the conversation in the drawing room. One more false, extraneous move, and the entire plan could fall apart.

To make sure no one forgot what they had to do, she showed the floor plan of the house to her team one more time, directing them with her finger to the spots, doors, and windows where they must set the fires.

The make-up artist was retouching the paint on the Peking opera singers' faces when Little Yin came in to tell them the audience was ready for their act to begin. The singers, all dressed now in their sparkly, elaborate costumes, went to take the stage along with the drummer and the three musicians.

Wen-Ying, still disguised in her make-up and wig, but dressed in an opera singer's white long-sleeved undershirt and white trousers, followed them to the door. She watched the performers and musicians walk through the corridor into the dining room, and caught Huang Jia-Ming peeking out from the kitchen door.

He gave her a hand signal to let her know his part of the operation would start right now. Wen-Ying nodded. Stealthily, he led two Tian Di Hui members, dressed as kitchen staff, out to the hallway and knocked on the door to the food storage closet. Three more members came out, all dressed in fake Japanese army uniforms.

Her pulse racing, Wen-Ying watched as Huang, with Ah Green in one of the fake uniforms following close behind him, went toward the servants' exit at the back while the others dispersed to different exits of the house. Huang opened the door. The Japanese guard outside barely turned his head before Huang shot a bullet into his temple. The guard fell and Huang quickly dragged his body inside into the food storage closet. Ah Green grabbed the soldier's rifle and took his place, then closed the back door.

A drip of sweat fell down the side of Wen-Ying's face. She raised her hand to wipe it away, then stopped when she remembered her face was covered with makeup. She took a deep breath instead. She must remain calm. Everything, including her makeup, must stay in place and on course.

"I'll go see if the others need help," Huang whispered as he passed her. From the dining room, the singing voices of the performers squealing their duet of a confession of love sounded surreal given the deadly tasks they were here to commit.

Her body tensed as a rock, Wen-Ying waited. She only had a brief moment to relax when she saw Huang and the other shooters return before the duet finished. Huang gave her a thumbs up and hurried back into the kitchen with his team. A round of applause resounded as Little Yin peeked out from the dining room and called for the *guqin* player, who was up next.

The woman who played the *guqin* stood up. As she exited the room, she paused and said to Wen-Ying, "It all depends on you now."

She didn't wait for Wen-Ying to respond. The Peking opera

singers and their accompanying musicians returned to the corridor and the *guqin* player went into the door from which they had come. Back in the room, the opera singers quickly shed their costumes. Leaving behind the drummer who still had to perform for the mask changer, they, the three musicians, the make-up artist, and the costume manager all headed to the servants' exit for their escape. Bao Gong, who had been watching everything from the kitchen door, waved his hand frantically at them and mouthed the word "hurry" as they passed by.

After they left, Huang and his team quietly began hauling out containers of kerosene. Wen-Ying signaled her team to come forward. Their turn was next.

The opening tunes of the *guqin* flowed from the dining room into the hallway. The second act had begun.

All at once, Wen-Ying felt propelled by the *guqin's* four tones: clear, ethereal, low, and far. Her footsteps in unison with the static, quiet beats. A musical instrument of scholars since the ancient days, the *guqin* conveyed sounds that could be grasped only by those with the highest minds.

Understanding the *guqin* posed no obstacle for her. After all, she was the daughter of the Yuan family. The Yuan children were brought up exposed to all four arts of a scholar: *guqin* music, the game of *go*, calligraphy, and painting.

For those who could understand it, *guqin* music would create a void. An empty realm where one's eyes would open and see clearly the complexities of nature and life in the vast universe. For everyone else, it would mesmerize and hypnotize. Its sounds could disarm them and put them under the zither's spell. Some said it could even deplete a weak mind and abandon it in a vacuum of delirium, if the performer intended harm.

In this void, Wen-Ying steered her team past the maze of rooms and the corridors, dousing fuel on floors and frames to create their labyrinth of death. In the dining room, the *guqin* kept its listeners still, encircling them in a musical wall and clouding their minds with forceful plucks of strings, dizzying vibrating chords, and haunting echoes. With the music shielding off the targets in another realm, Wen-Ying and her team carried on. All was going as planned. Even for Yu-Lan. Her delicate hands and slender arms never once gave in as she lifted the containers and poured the fluid of revenge to seal the enemy's fate.

As they closed their trap, the music's pace quickened, rising slowly at first but soon broke into a frenzy, high-pitched crescendo.

This was the end, Wen-Ying thought as she led everyone back to the sitting room. Her heart beating rapidly in synchrony to the staccato of pounding musical notes.

Another round of applause. The time had come for the final act.

The troupe leader, dressed in his vibrantly colored costume, cape, and headgear with a wildly painted mask over his face, rose for his turn. For his part tonight, he would play an ancient warrior.

And a true warrior he was, Wen-Ying thought. Being the performer of the last act, his role carried the highest risk. If he faltered, their whole plot would unravel and they would all be discovered. If that happened, they would all be killed. Until he finished his act, their lives were in his hands as much as Wen-Ying's.

He exchanged one grave, determined look with Wen-Ying before entering the dining room with the drummer.

At the servants' exit, Bao Gong silently urged the *guqin* player to leave.

"Thank you." Wen-Ying gave the woman her parting words. She firmly believed the *guqin's* music had given them a protective shield which guaranteed the completion of their second phase.

"Good luck and Heaven help us all." The woman picked up her instrument and vanished out the door into the dark.

With his team, Huang came out of the kitchen, bearing

lighters which they passed on to the rest in the sitting room. All the troupe's staff were gone now. Only Tian Di Hui members remained, waiting to carry out their final act.

The steady drumbeats began. Taking a calculated risk, Wen-Ying came to the door at the back of the dining room and peeked inside. With their backs toward the dining table and their attention focused on the performer, the audience inside did not know they were being watched. In the front, the mask changer marched in circles. His arm movements and steps in rhythm with the drum. With one, swift swing of his cape over his face, his white mask with yellow streaks on the cheeks vanished, replaced by a gray one with large purple eyes, thick black brows, and purple lips. Another toss of his head and the mask switched again, this time to one that was lime green painted to show an expression of arrogance. Matching his pace to the rolling drumbeats, he shuffled back, then lunged forward. An unexpected nod coupled with a blink of his eyes, and his mask changed again to one of blue with long lips painted in deep red curling upward into a wide grin. Even Kazuki raised his arms and clapped.

Behind the door in the back, Wen-Ying watched intently the mask changer's every move as he dazzled with the continuous alteration of faces. Multi-colored masks. Masks of sorrow, anger, surprise, and delight. Masks that looked like a monkey, wildcat, fox, ghosts, devils, and gods.

And then, it happened. The red mask. As soon as he switched, Takeda got up. Making as little disturbance as possible, he departed the room. The other audience's attention remained fixed on the mask changer.

Not missing a beat, Little Yin hopped to open the door for Takeda. In the process, she flashed a signal to the group waiting in the sitting room.

Immediately, Wen-Ying retreated away from the door and

rejoined her group. From the kitchen, faint films of smoke were already seeping out.

Huang shoved a handful more lighters into her palms. "Are you ready?"

"Yes." She dropped the lighters into the side pockets of her top. The opera singers' undergarment, it turned out, was perfect for what she needed.

"Be careful!" he said, then returned to the kitchen. In a few minutes, Bao Gong and his wife Ling would be hustling the household staff out under the claim of an accidental fire. Huang and Ah Green would pretend to volunteer to stay behind to put it out so they could convince the staff to leave. They would also set the door of the dining room afire as soon as the mask changer, the drummer, and Little Yin got out.

"This way," she said to the rest of her group. "We have ten minutes."

In the corridor, they spread out, each heading to the areas and rooms they were assigned to torch. Wen-Ying herself had chosen to burn the area deepest and farthest away from their escape route. This was what Fan Yong-Hao would have done. He would have placed himself in the spot with the most danger and risk, and he would see to it that everyone else was safe before he secured his own getaway. She intended to do the same.

Passing the front stairwell, she came face to face with Takeda returning from the direction of the washroom. He had gone that way to avoid raising suspicions and was now circling back.

Quickly, Wen-Ying grabbed his arm. "The servant's exit is back there. Get out now."

"No." He put his hand on the back of hers. "I'm going upstairs. I promised I'll get you a branch of the cypress tree, remember?"

The branch of the cypress tree? Was he joking? "Forget it," she said. "Just leave."

"I've got time." He smiled and pushed off her hand, then started upstairs.

"Takeda!" she called after him in a loud whisper. He gazed back down at her and smiled again, and continued his way up.

With no time to lose, Wen-Ying had no choice. She hurried to the front door and threw a lighter onto the kerosene fluid to set it ablaze. In the main drawing room, she burned the frame of every window. As the flames around her grew, she waited, listening for the drumbeats from the dining room to stop. Once the last performers got out, she would set afire the door connecting the drawing room to the dining room, shutting forever one of the three ways of escape for the beasts and demons trapped within.

The last round of applause came. A lighter in her hand, Wen-Ying stood. The heat now swelling around her. Switching on a lighter, she approached the fateful door. A bitter smile spread across her face. "You all can go to hell." She lit the lighter and threw it against the door doused with kerosene, yanking her hand back before the door burst into flame. To cut off all chances of escape, she lit another lighter and threw it into the pool of fuel at the bottom of the door.

A loud scream of a woman shot out from the other side. Tumbling footsteps, falling chairs, and desperate cries for help. Wen-Ying took a step backward, then another. It would all be over soon. After tonight, everything would turn to dissipating smoke and dispersing clouds.

Her job wasn't done yet. She turned around and traced her steps back. The curtains on the windows, the paintings on the wall, the wooden furniture, all were now caught in flame. The rising temperature would soon be unbearable. She needed to make sure all her Tian Di Hui brothers and sisters had escaped before the smoke began to suffocate.

Shrieks and shouts now filled the back of the house. She hustled through every room, slamming open each door to check and make sure none of her team was left behind. Sweat dripped from her scalp below her wig. She tore the wig off and flung it to the side. Perspiration soaked the shirt on her back. Her own sweat, mixed with the heavy paint and makeup she had put on to conceal herself, rolled down her eyes and cheeks. She wiped her forearm over her face. Blots of white, red, and black makeup came off, tainting her wide white sleeve.

"Get out!" she yelled at everyone she found who was looking to escape. Just as she'd thought, no one knew the ways around this house better than her. No one could've pointed the others to the quickest route to the only exit left which remained open to the outside.

"Yu-Lan!" She found her friend as she came upon the second doorway to the dining room.

"I did it!" Yu-Lan said. Her face convoluted in both joy and shock. "I sealed this doorway."

Wen-Ying wiped her sleeve across her face again. The cries for help inside prodded her conscience. Why? Weren't they only wails and screams of beasts? The heat. The fire. They were clouding her mind.

Biting back her instinct to heed their voices, Wen-Ying grabbed Yu-Lan's hand. "You have to get out. Now!"

Together, they ran toward the back. From her end of the corridor, Wen-Ying could see Bao Gong, his wife, and their daughter running outside under the moonlight. Beyond the servants' door leading to the garden, she could see shadows of the household staff who had escaped, still running for their lives.

"Go!" She pushed Yu-Lan ahead, then went to check the sitting room where they had gathered earlier to make sure that no one else was still inside.

Empty. Good. She ran toward the servants' exit. Huang was still there, waiting. "Hurry! Hurry!" he shouted to her.

Choking from the smoke, she asked him, "Is everyone out?"

"Yes. All our people are out."

"What about the servants and maids?"

"Don't know. I left that up to Bao Gong."

Nodding, she inhaled several deep breaths. Deep within the villa, the enemy and traitors continued their faint, dying cries for help.

"We can seal this door now." Huang held up a lighter.

"Wait." She clutched his hand. "Where's Takeda? Did he get out?"

A shade of hesitation colored his face. "He must have. He was one of the first who got to leave."

"Are you sure?" She shook his fist. "Did you see him leave with your own eyes?"

"No." Huang tightened his hand. "I was in the kitchen fanning the smoke pretending to put out the fire, remember?"

They stared at each other, uncertain what to do next.

Wen-Ying looked up the steps behind the back stairwell. Takeda couldn't still be up there, could he?

She turned her head and gazed out at the confusion and chaos in the backyard. The survivors were running everywhere for escape. Two dedicated servants even found buckets. They ran around, carrying the buckets, but could find no water.

Could Takeda be among the escapees? He had to be. Where else could he be? Pulling Huang's hand, Wen-Ying said, "Go see if he's out there. I'll wait. If you find him, come back at once and let me know. I'll seal this door then."

Huang pressed his lips. "All right." He gave her the lighter and ran toward the crowd.

At the door, Wen-Ying looked back inside. The flames had spread to the hallway. The flood of fire roared and sparks flew as smoke billowed upward. In a few minutes, this last passage to safety would close, whether she lit the fire to seal it or not.

Go up, a voice inside her urged. *Go up and make sure he's gone.*

Hearing that voice, she almost made a run for it. Even if it meant risking her own life. She braced her legs, ready to move. But another voice, the voice of duty, held her back. Their mission depended on her. She couldn't leave this final exit open and unattended.

Conflict roiled in her mind. Out of the haze of smoke, a figure appeared on top of the back stairway. Takeda! That fool!

No time to waste. "Takeda!" she shouted. "Hurry!"

He rushed down the stairs, waving a cypress branch full of leaves.

"Hurry!" she shouted again. As Takeda made his way down, another figure stumbled out from the other side of the corridor, flames burning on the back of his sleeves like small wings of fire.

The figure looked up. His eyes fixed on Wen-Ying standing at the door. "It's you! Yuan Wen-Ying!"

Tang Wei?

Wen-Ying's mouth dropped.

No! She wanted to scream. Or maybe she did scream. She could no longer tell. How? How did he get out?

"I'll kill you!" He made a mad dash forward.

No! The fire of rage erupted inside her, its blistering light blinding her to everything else except the traitor rushing head on toward her.

This beast. He would not get out. She wouldn't let him. She would make him pay for what he had done. "Mei Mei." She lit the lighter in her hand. "I avenge you now." With one swing, she chucked the lighter into the pool of kerosene by her feet.

Instantly, the flame burst. The waft of heat thrust her back. A ball of fire consumed the doorway. Behind the flares, Tang Wei's figure disappeared. Heaving her chest, Wen-Ying watched him burn.

Another voice called her name. "Wen-Ying!"

Startled, she looked up. "Takeda!"

What had she done?

"Takeda!" she cried at the top of her lungs. His face appeared and disappeared through the small opening between the flames. A face of shock and total loss of hope.

"No!" Wen-Ying shrieked. "Help!" She cried again. "Help!" She stepped forward, but could not break through. The wall of fire was sealed. No one could pass.

A wave of dizziness staggered her. Her legs weakened, she kneeled to the ground.

Behind her, Huang Jia-Ming and Zhang Yu-Lan ran to her side. "Wen-Ying! Wen-Ying!" They helped her up.

"Takeda!" She pointed at the burning door. "He's still inside."

Huang and Yu-Lan widened their eyes. Panic seized their faces.

"Takeda!" Wen-Ying cried out again.

Huang looked at the door, then at her. "We have to go." He grimaced and tossed his head at Yu-Lan. "The getaway car is waiting. We have to leave."

"Wen-Ying." Yu-Lan pulled her by the arm. " Let's go."

Wen-Ying could not think. The fire had sapped every bit of energy out of her body. The rage that consumed her before had burned out, and pain was all that was left. Raw, searing pain as she had never felt in her life.

Propping her up by the arm on each side, Huang and Yu-Lan pulled her toward the silent vehicle waiting across the street in the dark.

Sirens wailed as they dragged her away. In a stupor, Wen-Ying turned back her head. "Masao," she whimpered. Useless tears rained down her face. "Zheng-Xiong," she repeated his name. "Zheng-Xiong."

But he could not hear her. He would never answer again no matter what name she called him.

The fire continued to burn. The villa, once grand and illustrious, now glowed like a giant inferno, basking in its last triumphant light. Helpless, Wen-Ying gazed up. High above in the sky, the moon beamed, casting her own shadow over her path. Her feet followed, but the shadow remained forever one step ahead.er

Chang 'e, that daring heroine who made the impulsive move to drink the elixir of immortality to thwart the treachery of Feng Meng. That celestial goddess who ascended the heaven to chase the moon, leaving behind her love Hou Yi to chase her shadow for all his remaining days. What words of wisdom would she give to those who must follow her path, when soul-shattering sacrifices must be made for the night to restore its peace for the days and years ahead?

The Moon Chaser is a spin-off story from the *Shanghai Story* trilogy, a WWII drama saga based on Clark Yuan, Wen-Ying's older brother, and Eden Levine, the Jewish refugee from Munich who escaped to Shanghai with her family.

Get your copy on Amazon to find out more.

Author's Note: To see a mask changing performance after a Chinese feast, watch Anthony Bourdain's *Parts Unknown,* Season 8, Episode 3, when he visited Sichuan with Eric Ripert.

Enjoyed reading my stories?

Subscribe for a free story

On his last night in New York, a young grifter sets out to turn the table on those who shorted him before he leaves for the draft. Will he win or lose?

Sign up for my mailing list and receive a free copy of another spin-off story from the ***Rose of Anzio*** series, ***Christmas Eve in the City of Dreams***, plus news on book releases, free stories, and more.

ttp://alexakang.com/akangnews2/

Shanghai Story Trilogy
By Alexa Kang

Available on Amazon
Read Free on Kindle Unlimited

Book One - Shanghai Story
Book Two - Shanghai Dreams
Book Three - Shanghai Yesterday

ABOUT THE AUTHOR

Alexa Kang is a WWII and 20th century historical fiction author. Her works include the novel series, *Rose of Anzio,* a love story saga that begins in 1940 Chicago and continues on to the historic Battle of Anzio in Italy. Her second series, *Shanghai Story,* chronicles the events in Shanghai leading up to WWII and the history of Jews and Jewish refugees in China. Her other works include the WWII/1980s time-travel love story *Eternal Flame* (a tribute to John Hughes), as well as short stories in the fiction anthologies *Pearl Harbor and More: Stories of December 1942, Christmas in Love,* and the USA Today Bestseller *The Darkest Hour*.

Get in Touch!

I would love to hear from you.

Contact me or follow me at:

www.alexakang.com

alexa@alexakang.com

You can also find me on Facebook and BookBub

Also by Alexa Kang

The Rose of Anzio Series

*A sweeping saga of love and war, **Rose of Anzio** takes you from 1940s Chicago to the WWII Battle of Anzio in Italy and beyond.*

Book One ~ Moonlight

Book Two ~ Jalousie

Book Three ~ Desire

Book Four ~ Remembrance

New Release

Nisei War Series Book One

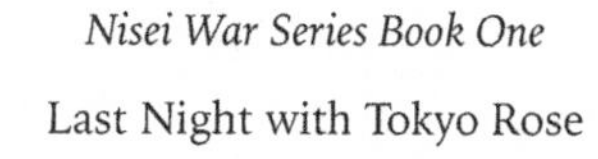

Last Night with Tokyo Rose

Official Release Date: January 22, 2021

Get your copy now on Amazon

Read free on Kindle Unlimited